HAROLD SONNY LADOO was born in Trinidad in 1945, the son of a peasant. He grew up in the Caribbean, working in the cane fields and on the boats. In 1968 he immigrated to Toronto, Canada with his wife and two children, and enrolled at Erindale College at the University of Toronto. He maintained a double life, studying and writing by day and working by night in a variety of restaurant jobs in order to support his family. In 1972 he graduated with a BA and in September House of Anansi Press published his first novel, *No Pain Like This Body*. This earned Ladoo immediate recognition as a new literary talent and he was awarded a writing bursary from the Canada Council which he used to finance his return to Trinidad in August 1973, to research further books. His trip was tragically curtailed when on 17 August he was discovered in a drainage ditch, having been brutally attacked. He died shortly afterwards, aged just 28.

His second novel, *Yesterdays*, was published posthumously in 1974, and Canada lamented again the loss of a gifted writer. Harold Sonny Ladoo left behind him a large collection of manuscripts: two further novels, many short stories and poems.

for

Peter Such

Dennis Lee

Shirley Gibson

No Pain
Like This Body

a Novel

Harold Sonny Ladoo

Introduction by
Dionne Brand

ANANSI

First published in 1972 by House of Anansi Press Ltd.

This edition published in 2003 by
House of Anansi Press Inc.
110 Spadina Ave., Suite 801
Toronto, ON, M5V 2K4
Tel. 416-363-4343
Fax 416-363-1017
www.anansi.ca

Distributed in Canada by
Publishers Group Canada
250A Carlton Street
Toronto, ON, M5A 2L1
Tel. 416-934-9900
Toll free order numbers:
Tel. 800-663-5714
Fax 800-565-3770

07 06 05 04 03   1 2 3 4 5

NATIONAL LIBRARY OF CANADA CATALOGUING IN PUBLICATION DATA

Ladoo, Harold Sonny, 1945–1973
No pain like this body / Harold Sonny Ladoo ; introduction by Dionne Brand.

Publ. originally 1972.
ISBN 0-88784-689-0

I. Title.

PS8573.A28N6 2003   C813'.54   C2003-900535-6
PR9199.3.L277N6 2003

Cover design: Bill Douglas at The Bang
Typesetting: Brian Panhuyzen

**Canada Council   Conseil des Arts
for the Arts   du Canada**

*We acknowledge for their financial support of our publishing program the Canada Council
for the Arts, the Ontario Arts Council, and the Government of Canada through the Book
Publishing Industry Development Program (BPIDP).*

Printed and bound in Canada.

There is no fire like passion;
there is no losing throw like hatred;
there is no pain like this body;
there is no happiness higher than rest.

— *The Dhammapada*

INTRODUCTION

I

"THOUGH ONE SHOULD LIVE a hundred years not seeing the Truth Sublime, yet better, indeed, is a single day's life of one who sees the Truth Sublime."

If you came from the same place as Harold Sonny Ladoo, you were likely to think, as he probably did, that books held the possibility of changing your life, that they could take you to other places, that they could free you of any reality, that reading them was not an impassive act, that the person who entered them was not the same person who emerged from them, that they changed some tissue in the brain, revealed some truth that clarified your condition, and that rescued you, and that the best of them called you into a communion with other human beings against solitude, against torment, against misery. You were likely a boy or a girl walking a rice paddy or a cane field or a cluttered street or a crowded yard suspended by a kind of joy that emanated from the half-read book under your arm; you likely forgot some parental order, stumbled on a stone, spilled precious water or milk in the thought that someone had so precisely put the person you thought you were in a book. Or that they had gotten it so wrong, nevertheless, that when you could, you would do it yourself; and, when you had, someone else walking along in the same way would be equally suspended by the sublime truth of it. Harold Sonny Ladoo's *No Pain Like This Body* has all the gritty concentration of such an experience.

II

I went to school with Ladoo. I did not know him except in the nodding acknowledgement one makes at impromptu gatherings of people who think that they are or ought to be associated by race or country of origin or some recognized affinity through colonialism. People who are thrown together find each other through accent, geography, cosmic accident or what Caribbean writer Wilson Harris called the great heterogeneity of the New World. I sensed in Ladoo a reluctance, a skepticism as well as an acknowledgement of that affinity. One could not blame him, since these affinities are never primarily occasions of joy. They assume too much about personality even as they offer solidarity, even as they seek to revive lost spirits.

Ladoo seemed to me, in the glimpses I had of him in the two years we attended Erindale College together at the University of Toronto, a brooding unhappy man. He smoked continually, his cheeks sucked into chasms cut out of a bony face, a permanent scowl etched there by the hard place he had come from in Trinidad, a place called McBean; mistrustful eyes made so no doubt by the same harsh landscape of subsistence agriculture he had hacked his way out of with a few others. A dismissive turn to his equally bony compact body, he occupied the farthest corner of a room in the cafeteria that we, a cosmopolitan group calling itself the African-Asian West Indian Association, had taken over, or liberated, as we used to say. Ladoo sat there in a cloud of cigarette smoke working on *No Pain Like This Body*.

By turns he would be involved in vociferous arguments about some philosophical point with the rest of us, but mainly with Lennox Sankersingh, whom we all called Chorros. I never approached Ladoo, never to my recollection had any meaningful exchange with him. We others, with our mix of pan-colonial desires, political awakenings, and unbridled ambitions, left him to his writing, sometimes giving it the respect of a sacred act, sometimes grumbling and arguing with him about what seemed Ladoo's disengagement with what we considered real and urgent political issues. We were going to liberate the world and how could he be writing a mere book? He didn't care. He poured all his desires into that one line of the Dhammapada – the verses uttered by the Buddha: "There is no pain like this body." But despite our chiding, that line and Ladoo's passion for it was understandable to us. Not only in the philosophical sense. We had experienced its practical meanings. For although he ignored us, and some would have said disdained us, he was with us. We knew him to be cutting out a particular figure recognizable to all of us in its sovereign agonies. For where had he come from if not from the same latitude of flung identities. That line's brutal ministration was as familiar to us as our families and the skies and earth we open our eyes to each morning. Indeed it gave our situations a grace, a connection with the eternal, and, albeit unchangeable, a license to do what one could. At least that was my interpretation at the time. Romantic, perhaps fatalist.

III

And there was another Ladoo. We called him Plato jokingly. He was given the nickname by Chorros. A nickname he acknowledged, relished, possibly because in the thick of tobacco smoke, his face older than its years, he would argue any point with vigour and intensity. The room in the cafeteria at Erindale was full of discussions on Fanon, Sartre, Marcuse, Marx, C. L. R. James, Angela Davis, Lenin and Mao. Ladoo liked the idea of being compared to Plato in these battles. Most of us knew him only by this name.

Plato and Chorros got into many an argument, the rest of us bringing up the rear. One particular fight was over V. S. Naipaul. Plato argued that he was a better writer than Naipaul, and Chorros being a logician asked him how he had come to that conclusion and could he measure it scientifically. Plato exploded, grabbing hold of Chorros, at which point our room in the cafeteria went uncharacteristically silent. Suddenly, referring to Chorros' broken-down car, Plato said, "Hey Chorros, how the Volkswagen going?" The violence of the moment diffused.

We heard of other violent moments in his life at home, though we were never privy to those. Ladoo was an intense man. He saw his mission on par with Naipaul and Sam Selvon. He had, as Chorros reminded me, little patience for things not directly related to himself and that mission. In his late teens when he found himself without a formal education, he and several friends decided to study independently for the Cambridge O-level exams. They formed a group and pushed each other, met, staying up nights after work cramming until they were successful. On the strength of which Ladoo and others in the group immigrated to Canada (one of Ladoo's colleagues is now a minister in the Trinidad government). Ladoo applied that same grit to writing. He spent sleepless nights writing around job and school and family. He had scraped himself up from a hardscrabble place and was determined to become a great writer. And he was at the beginning of that mission when he was killed. Plato did not die in old age like his namesake, but like the small protagonist of his novel he perished from place and arbitrary violence. That hardscrabble village he had come from embraced him again, and that last time he was unable to escape.

<h2 style="text-align:center">IV</h2>

The Caribbean is a place of infinite reinvention. How else Naipaul, Walcott, Marley Brodber, Conde, Carpentier and Wynter. How else son, reggae, calypso, steel pan, zouk. How else Marcus Garvey and C. L. R. James. All recreations, recombinations of ancestral memory, harsh New World reality and undaunted imagination.

There was a road I travelled when I was a child. I only remember it from the vantage point of a child, eye level to the side window of a moving car or receding backward through the rear window. It was a road and journey that began in excitement and anticipation but that under the weight of the landscape ended in what seemed dreadful days later with existential nausea. This was the road from San Fernando to Guayguayare. The road passed through the towns of Princes Town, Rio Claro, Tableland and Mayaro. These were the main towns, the sign posts of progression to either end. In between and for miles on end there was nothing. Except endless fields of sugar cane relentlessly waving, by turns striking the air like the Goddess Durga and by turns seeming a blue-green ocean, a manifestation of the goddess Yemaya — both having made the crossing and assembled on this island from the Old Worlds of India and Africa. Boredom and sickliness affected the traveller here, a loneliness sprang up along the road and a grim drudgery.

Somewhere off the road was a place aptly called the Devil's

Woodyard. The eternal fields of cane were interrupted here and there by red, white and yellow jhandis – Hindu prayer flags signalling a dwelling, a devotee, a brilliant faith that had survived the arduous crossing from India. Once in a while along the empty road a woman with an orhni over her head or a girl carrying water stunned momentarily by the car would stare. The car dizzily swerving, the driver, a man named Dillon, stirring from the monotony of the road at the surprise of other humans.

Secreted off this road there were traces and villages hacked out of the cane; places that African forced labour had despairingly abandoned and where Indian people had been brought two generations before as indentured labourers. An equally despairing endeavour. The feeling all along these traces, in these villages, was mournful, a patient brooding. Their grim sense repeating and multiplying in other places called Barrackpore, Penal, Balmain, Fyzabad, Felicity, Calcutta, Palmyra, and McBean through which Ladoo observed the same desperation. Something living in them like the past and yet something waiting to be invented. One could either make something of these places or be crushed by them. And for all the marvellous turns of imagination that allow people to survive history's arbitrariness, one is not always able to rise to the task of reinvention, one is not always successful at it. One fails. Ladoo's *No Pain Like This Body* tells of just such a failure. The novel is a Veda to the beginnings of Indian life in Trinidad. Life in the not so imaginary Tola Trace. A life of the barest subsistence and what must have seemed abandonment by the gods. Ladoo by this act, by the writing of a hymn to these origins, thought that he could reinvent himself. And he did, momentarily. His early death cutting his work short.

V

In the ancient text the Ramayana, Rama is wrongfully sent into exile from Ayodhya. He spends fourteen years fighting various battles, the most crucial to reclaim his wife, Sita, from the demon king of Lanka, Ravana and he returns in triumph to Ayodhya to sit as its rightful king. On his return the people light deyas along his way welcoming him home. That epic myth arrived in the diaspora with indenture workers. It was perhaps a source of sustenance throughout their own exile. A return garlanded in the lights of welcome awaited them after the bleak drudgery of a life tied to plantations of cane and rice.

This epic lies somewhere in the text of *No Pain Like This Body*. But no garland of lights precedes or follows Ladoo's Rama. A fever burns in him, he is stung by scorpions and eventually carried even farther away from mythic Ayodhya. The lights that preceded Rama were supposed to remove darkness not only from homes but also to banish ignorance and hatred from hearts. Ladoo renders a Ramayana steeped in hatred and violence. Plagued by incessant rain ("the rain fell like a shower of poison over Tola") and a god terrible and indifferent ("God does only eat and drink in that sky"), Ladoo's onomatopoeic insistencies make more horrifying the action in the novel. His characters' trusting innocence, their supplication to fate are made more disastrous by his feats of verbal play. Told through the view of a child, nature and human beings are overwhelmingly brutal.

VI

"Better than a thousand verses, comprising useless words, is one beneficial single line, by hearing which one attains peace."

These words uttered by the Buddha possibly describe Harold Ladoo's contribution to both Caribbean and Canadian literature. How can I say this of a novel so unrelentingly brutal. Because *No Pain Like This Body* is a novel that strips its reader of sentimentality of any kind – pity or superiority. It is a novel unconcerned with anything but truth-telling. And because peace is nothing without the truth, I suspect for Ladoo this was obvious. So much of his life had been spent in truth's bald presence that he was able to capture it in his brief time.

— Dionne Brand
March 2003

TOLA TRACE

August, 1905

CARIB ISLAND

Area: 1000 square miles.

History: Discovered by Columbus in 1498. Taken over by the British in 1797. East Indians came to Carib Island to work on the sugar plantations from 1845 to 1917.

Chief Exports: Sugar, petroleum, rum, cocoa, coffee, citrus fruits and asphalt.

(Also see Glossary)

TOLA DISTRICT – CARIB ISLAND

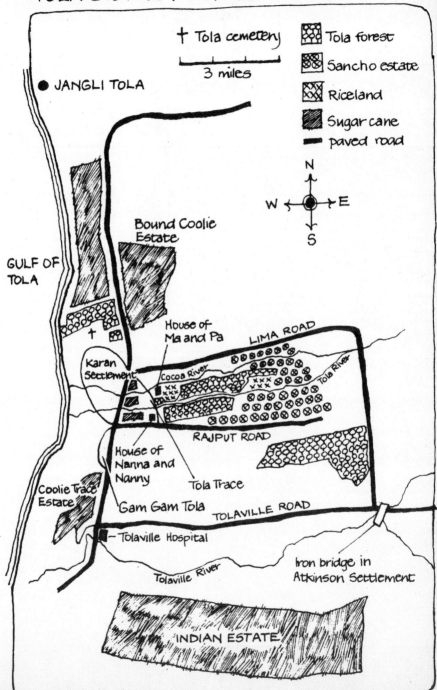

Tola cemetery

3 miles

Tola forest
Sancho estate
Riceland
Sugar cane
paved road

JANGLI TOLA

N
W ← → E
S

Bound Coolie Estate

GULF OF TOLA

House of Ma and Pa

LIMA ROAD

Cocoa River

Tola River

Karan Settlement

RAJPUT ROAD

House of Nanna and Nanny

Tola Trace

Coolie Trace Estate

Gam Gam Tola

TOLAVILLE ROAD

Tolaville Hospital

Iron bridge in Atkinson Settlement

Tolaville River

INDIAN ESTATE

I

PA CAME HOME. He didn't talk to Ma. He came home just like a snake. Quiet.

The rain was drizzling. Streaks of lightning like long green snakes wriggled against the black face of the sky. Balraj, Sunaree, Rama and Panday were in the riceland, not far from where Ma was washing clothes. The riceland began about ten feet away from the tub. Balraj was trying hard to catch the tadpoles; they were black black, black like rain clouds, and they were moving like spots of tar in the water. Balraj was the oldest. He was twelve. He tried hard like hell to catch the tadpoles and put them in the ricebag. But the tadpoles were smart, smarter than Balraj. They behaved like drunk people in the water; they were giving a lot of trouble; they kept running and running in the water; they had no legs, but they were running in the muddy water; just running and running away from Balraj. Balraj wanted to catch the tadpoles so he kept on running behind them; and they knew that Balraj wanted to put them inside the ricebag, so they ran all the time away from him.

Sunaree was ten years old. She was dragging the ricebag in the water, just behind Balraj. But Balraj was getting fed up. The tadpoles were hiding away from him.

Rama and Panday were eight years old. Twins. They were naked. Both of them were running behind Sunaree. As they ran they kicked up water and soiled Sunaree's dress. Sunaree turned around. She was vexed and her face looked like a rain cloud. Then she said, "Now Rama and Panday behave all you self!"

While she was talking to Rama and Panday, Balraj dragged his hands in the water to catch the tadpoles. He lifted his hands out. There were about ten tadpoles inside them. They were trying to jump out of his hands and go back into the water. Balraj turned around to put the tadpoles in the ricebag. Sunaree was not paying attention; she had the bag in the water, and she was talking to Rama and Panday. Balraj got mad; he bawled out, "Sunaree I goin to kick you! Where de bag is?"

"De bag in de wadder bredder."

"Wot it doin in de wadder?"

"It not doin notten."

"Well pick up dat bag and open it."

"Oright."

Sunaree had a great love for the tadpoles also, so she opened the ricebag. Balraj dropped the crappo fish inside the ricebag, and bent down in the water again.

Rama and Panday walked up to Sunaree. They were not walking easy as a fly walks; they were walking like mules; feet went *splunk splunk splunk* in the water.

"Rama and Panday all you walk easier dan dat," Balraj told them. "Dese crappo fish smart like hell. Wen dey hear all you walkin hard hard dey go run away."

Rama and Panday didn't listen to Balraj. They held on to the ricebag. They opened it and peeped inside the bag. Their eyes were bulging like ripe guavas; they were trying hard to see the tadpoles that were in the bag, but they could not see anything. Rama sucked his teeth and said, "I want to go in dat bag."

Sunaree told him he couldn't go inside the ricebag, because he was going to kill the tadpoles.

"I want to go in dat bag too," Panday declared.

"But I say all you cant go in dat bag. All you goin to kill de fish."

Rama and Panday tried to pull the ricebag away from Sunaree. She was talking and begging them not to pull the bag; crying and begging them not to pull it away; crying not for her sake but for the tadpoles' sake, because she wanted the crappo fish to live. But Rama and Panday pulled the bag away from her.

Balraj walked in the water. His back was bent as if he was an old man. He knew that the tadpoles were smart, so he watched them carefully. There were some crappo fish near the bamboo grass; there were hundreds of them; they were dancing and moving like a patch of blackness. Balraj walked quietly. He moved closer to them; they did not see him, because they were dancing in a group. He bent down. Slowly. He stretched his hands. Then *wash wash* his hands swept through the water. He turned around to put the tadpoles in the ricebag. Balraj just turned around and dropped them inside the bag. But there was no bag; the tadpoles fell back into the water. Balraj just stood and looked and looked at the tadpoles that were free again in the water, then he got mad like a bull. He looked. Rama and Panday were dragging the bag in the water.

"Wot de hell all you doin wid dat bag?"

"We just playin bredder," Panday said.

"Now all you drop dat bag!"

Balraj couldn't control himself. He ran up to them just like a horse. Rama and Panday dropped the bag in the water and started running towards the cashew tree.

Sunaree saw Balraj coming like a jackspaniard. She did not know what to do, so she just stood there and stared at Balraj.

"Why you give dem two son of a bitches dat bag?"

"I not give dem it."

"Den who give dem it?"

"I tell you dey take it deyself."

Sunaree had long black hair; it was thick like grass. Balraj grabbed her hair and started kicking her in the water. She pushed Balraj, and he fell *splash* in the water. Sunaree wanted to run away, but she couldn't run away; Balraj grabbed her hair again; he was pulling her hair as if he was going to pull out her head. Then he started dragging her in the muddy water.

Balraj couldn't see Pa at all. Pa just stood in the banana patch like a big snake and watched all the time. Ma was busy washing the clothes; she couldn't see Pa either. Pa was just hiding and watching with poison in his eyes. Ma was just washing the clothes under the plum tree. Her back was bent low over the tub, and she was washing as if the clothes were rottening with dirt; she just bent over the tub and scrubbed like a crazy woman. Then she heard Sunaree bawling. Ma lifted her head. Balraj was still dragging Sunaree in the water.

Ma shouted, "Leggo dat chile Balraj!"

"I not lettin she go!"

"Boy I is you modder. I make you. You just lissen to me. Leggo she."

"I not lettin she go!"

"I comin in dat wadder for you right now Balraj!"

Ma was fed up. She washed out her hands in the soapy water. Then she walked to the edge of the riceland. Ma was quarrelling and pointing at Balraj. Suddenly she stood up. She saw Pa. Ma turned around and walked back to the tub.

Pa came out of the banana patch.

"Now all you chirens come outa dat wadder!" he shouted.

Pa had a voice like thunder. When he spoke the riceland shook as if God was shaking up Tola.

Rama and Panday were near the cashew tree. They were trying to hold the mamzels, but they moved like the wind.

"Let we catch dem crabs," Rama suggested.

"And do wot wid dem?" Panday asked.

"Kill dem."

"It not good to kill notten."

They had to be careful in the riceland. There were deep holes all over the place, especially near the cashew and barahar trees. The holes were not deep like a well or a river, but they were deep enough to drown Rama and Panday.

"It have crabs near dat barahar tree," Rama said.

"It too deep by de barahar tree," Panday told him.

"It not too deep. Dem red crabs livin in dem holes."

"But dem holes deep deep."

"I still goin to walk to de barahar tree," Rama declared.

Rama began walking eastwards across the riceland. Panday was begging him not to go, but Rama was not listening; he was harden like a goat. But Rama couldn't go. He and Panday heard when Pa shouted at Balraj and Sunaree. Panday and Rama ran out of the riceland, passed through the banana patch and went by the rainwater barrel. The rainwater barrel was almost touching the tapia wall at the eastern side of the house.

When Pa shouted, Balraj released Sunaree. She ran out of the riceland, passed Ma by the tub and went and joined Rama and Panday by the rainwater barrel, but Balraj remained inside the riceland. He stood up and looked at Pa; he was watching as if he was going to eat Pa; he was really playing man for Pa. Pa made an attempt to go in the water. Balraj was afraid; he ran to the eastern side of the riceland. He ran as fast as a cloud moves in the sky. Then he stood up on a meri on the other side of the riceland and looked at Pa.

"Now Balraj come outa dat wadder!"

"I fraid you beat me."

"I not goin to do you notten boy."

"Oright."

Pa was smarter than a snake; he began to talk soft as if a child was talking. He said that he was not going to beat Balraj, because he was a child. He thought that Pa was talking the truth; he began to walk to meet him. Pa just stood there and looked at him; just stood on the edge of the riceland and waited as a snake.

Balraj walked slowly. His feet didn't go *splash splash* in the water; they went *splunk* and *splunk* and then *splunk* as if a little child was walking in the water. He watched Pa with fear in his eyes as he came closer to the western edge of the riceland. Pa wasn't backward; he was watching Balraj with snaky eyes. The wind was blowing cold cold. Balraj was trembling. His teeth went *clax clax clax*. The wind was blowing from the north. It was cold as ice cream, and Balraj was trembling and watching Pa. The sky was black as Sunaree's hair, and Pa was watching Balraj. Balraj was almost out of the water. Pa leaned over the edge of the riceland and tried to hold his hand. Balraj ran *splash splash*. Pa ran eastwards along the riceland bank; his feet went *tats tats tats*. There were many snakes in the riceland; they lived inside the deep holes near the barahar tree. Balraj was trying to keep away from the holes, because he was afraid of the snakes. Balraj was tired running. He just stood in the water and looked at Pa. Pa was mad. He jumped up and down on the riceland bank.

"Balraj come outa dat wadder!" Pa shouted.

"I fraid you beat me."

"Boy com outa dat wadder!"

Balraj was afraid. He knew Pa was going to beat him real bad. *Crax crax cratax doom doommm doomed!* the thunder rolled. Balraj looked at the sky; it was blacker than a dream of

snakes and evil spirits. Pa bent down and picked up dirt from
the riceland bank. He started to pelt Balraj. Balraj was moving
from side to side trying hard to get away from the dirt. Pa
couldn't hit him. Pa was in a rage; he was pelting as a madman. Then Pa shouted, "Now come outa dat wadder boy! I
goin to pelt inside dem snake holes."

Balraj made no effort to come out of the riceland. Pa kept
pelting dirt into the deep holes. The water was bubbling and
bubbling and bubbling; bubbling and bubbling as if it was
boiling over with rage; it was boiling and bubbling as when a
ricepot bubbles over a fireside, but Balraj just stood there and
looked at Pa.

"You feel you is a big man?" Pa asked him.

"No."

"Den come outa dat wadder!"

"I fraid you beat me."

"Den you is a big man?"

"No. I is a little little chile. Little little."

"Well I goin to make a snake bite you ass!"

It was August, the middle of the rainy season. The rain was
falling and falling and falling as if the sky was leaking or something. Sunaree, Rama and Panday were still by the rainwater
barrel. Sunaree was holding the enamel dipper, but it slipped
from her hand and fell in the yard. The dipper was dirty; full of
mud all over. Rama and Panday were still naked. Trembling.

"I feelin cold."

"Hush else Pa go bust you liver wid a kick," Rama said.

"Pa stupid," Panday declared.

"Pa stupid like God."

"Now God have big eyes and he seein wot all you doin,"
Sunaree said.

"Somebody shouda hit God one kick and bust he eye!"
Rama shouted.

Sunaree told Rama that God had great big eyes; God never winked; even if dirt or flies or smoke went into his eyes, he never winked; God never slept or drank or ate; he never sheltered with a leaf from the wind and the rain; he just lived in heaven and stared at the earth all the time.

And Rama: "Den God like a stone. He just like a stone I tell you."

"You mean dat God does see wen Rama pee on me in de night?" Panday asked.

"Yeh," Sunaree said.

Sunaree picked up the enamel dipper, rinsed it inside the rainwater barrel, and said, "Now Rama and Panday come on inside dat house." She walked in front, and they followed her.

Balraj was still watching Pa; he was trembling like a banana leaf, but he was watching Pa. Pa was strong like a mango tree, so his teeth were not going *clax clax clax*, because he was not feeling cold.

Ma finished washing the clothes. She put them in the old bucket. She looked. Balraj was still inside the riceland. Ma said to Pa, "Dat chile fraid you. I bleed blood to make dat chile. Dat chile come from my belly after I carry him for nine monts. Now you let dat chile come outa dat wadder. I bleed blood to make dat chile!"

Pa spoke like a stone rolling down from a hill, "Now you just shut you kiss me ass mout woman! Shut it!"

Ma talked back as water falling from a house roof. She complained that Pa was not acting as a father at all. Pa had no heart because he was running Balraj in the riceland. She threatened that if anything happened to Balraj in the water, she was going to walk the three miles to Tolaville; walk the three miles just to get a policeman to lock up Pa.

"Kiss me ass!" Pa shouted.

And Ma talked again; she talked as a spider that is full of

poison. Pa hated the way she talked. He began to pelt more dirt into the water. The water was still bubbling. Pa aimed carefully. He threw the dirt. It fell *plunk* inside one of the deep holes. A huge water snake came to the surface of the muddy water.

Balraj started to run in the water. The snake moved *clips clips clips*. Fast. Faster. The snake moved as oil on the water. Balraj knew that the snake was chasing him, so he didn't look back. The snake went just a little way and turned back. But Balraj thought that the snake was following him; he ran out of the riceland and went by Ma. It was only when he reached by Ma that he looked back. There was no snake.

Pa was serious. He ran by the tub. There was not a laugh or a smile on his face; he just came by the tub to beat Balraj.

"Behave youself and leff me son alone!" Ma shouted.

"Shut you kiss me ass mout woman!"

Pa held Ma real hard beside the tub; he was pulling her; just pulling and pulling as if he was uprooting a sapodilla tree. Ma held on to Balraj, and he was holding on to the hog plum tree. Pa tried his best to kick Balraj, but Ma was in his way. Pa was sweating and blowing. "I goin to drownd you in dat tub woman!"

"Balraj is a little chile. You is a big man. You have no right to make a snake run him in dat wadder. But it have a God and he watchin from dat sky."

"God coud kiss me ass!"

"Well wen a man coud cuss God he deserve to dead!"

Pa hated Ma and he hated Balraj, so he picked up Ma as if he was picking up a little child and he held her in the air. Ma bawled like a cow hard hard hard. She tried to hold the hog plum tree, but she couldn't meet it. Ma didn't want to go inside the tub; she was turning and twisting as a worm; just turning and twisting and bawling; just bawling and trying to get away. The water in the tub was full of soap suds. Pa held her high, and he held her tight as a tree holds another tree. Ma was bawling and getting on; getting on and calling God, but the sky was black and God was only watching with his big eyes from heaven; he was not even trying to help Ma a little. Pa turned her over and pushed her face inside the tub; trying hard to drown her like. Her feet were high in the air, and her whole body was shaking as a banana leaf shakes when the wind blows.

Balraj got his chance. He ran by the rainwater barrel. But Balraj was confused. He didn't know where to run. He just stood by the rainwater barrel behind the house, and stared at Pa.

Then Pa changed his mind. He took Ma out of the tub. She coughed and coughed and coughed. She could not stand. She fell, got up, then she fell again. She rolled on the ground and vomited the soapy water.

Pa left Ma alone. He ran about twenty feet and came by the rainwater barrel. Balraj saw Pa coming but he couldn't move. Pa grabbed him by the barrel and struck him with his right hand. Balraj was not a man; he was not strong like a carat tree; he was just a boy, so the blow flattened him. Pa held his feet and dragged him away from the rainwater barrel. Balraj was bawling and rolling like a pig. Pa stood on his chest and told him to shut up.

Ma was still vomiting, but when she saw Pa standing on his chest, she got up. And Pa was not standing on Balraj's chest alone; he was standing on his chest and saying, "I go bust you liver today!" Pa was squeezing his chest real hard, and Balraj was bawling and bawling.

Ma ran up to Pa like a rat. Pa couldn't see her coming, his back was turned. She gave a good push; he almost fell over. Still standing on Balraj's chest, Pa threw a blow at her head. It sounded *biff!* as when a dry coconut falls. Then Pa picked up Balraj as a wet bundle of grass and threw him splash inside the drain. Pa turned around. He was looking for Ma. She ran past the rainwater barrel and went by the outhouse. Pa ran through the banana patch, but before he reached the out-house she ran westward, crossed Tola Trace and went inside the sugarcane field.

Balraj got up from the canal. He looked. Pa was still by the outhouse. He ran to the front of the house. He looked. Pa was coming through the banana patch again. Balraj dashed across Tola Trace and hid in the sugarcane field.

Sunaree, Rama and Panday were inside the house. Trem-bling. They peeped through the wide creases in the earthen wall. They saw Ma running and bawling; they saw her cross Tola Trace; they saw Balraj too; they saw him as he ran as a madman inside the sugarcane field. They wanted to run out of the house too, but they were afraid. Pa was walking up and down in the backyard as a crazy man. They were quiet in the house, just looking at him; looking and praying to God to keep Pa away from the house. Pa fished out a bottle of rum from his pocket and took a good drink. He drank out all and threw the flask away; it broke *splinks!* Sunaree, Rama and Panday were joined together in a living heap. They peeped through the creases again; Pa was walking towards the rice-land. A streak of lightning danced inside the house.

"Hide de dipper Panday!" Sunaree screamed.

"I fraid like hell to move from where I standin up."

"Hide dat dipper befo de lightnin cut out you tongue."

"I fraid I tell you!"

Sunaree took the dipper and flung it under the settee.

"Why God not kill dat lightnin ass?" Rama asked.

"Quiet befo dat lightnin hear you and cut out you tongue!" Sunaree told him.

They peeped through the creases again. Pa was standing under the barahar tree.

"God go care for we," Panday said.

"Dat is true bredder."

But Rama: "God does only eat and drink in dat sky."

"God go give you sin. Wen you dead de Devil go ride you like a horse in de night," Sunaree said.

They peeped through the creases again. Pa was walking back to the house.

"Let we run outa dis house fast!" Sunaree shouted.

They were ready; Rama and Panday were ready; they were naked and they were ready to run out of the house. Sunaree held their hands as they dashed out of the house. They ran across the yard into Tola Trace. They faced south, because they were running to meet the house of Nanna and Nanny in Rajput Road; they ran fast, because Nanna and Nanny lived half a mile away at the corner of Tola Trace and Rajput Road. Lightning jumped out of the clouds as green snakes and gold fishes, and the thunder shook up the whole of Tola, yet they didn't stop running. Dark clouds were coming closer to the earth like a black spider with a huge body, yet they kept on running. They ran, because they were sure that God was watching them with his big big eyes.

II

Sunaree, Rama and Panday ran down Tola Trace. Their feet went *flip flop flip flop* as if mules were running. The mud jumped up as little crickets and fell in the grass *toots toots*. The large holes in the trace were covered with muddy water. They had to watch carefully for the holes, because some of them were very deep. Panday was running good good, but he stopped suddenly. "Me belly hurtin me, Sunaree."

"Look Panday, run faster. If you run fast fast dat pain goin to past."

"But me belly hurtin real bad."

"You just run more fast."

"Oright."

Panday kept on running. Suddenly he stopped again. He stood upright as a carat tree. Sunaree and Rama asked him why he was standing; he said that he couldn't run any more.

"Why?" she asked him.

"Because I messup!"

Panday was smelling stink. He asked Sunaree and Rama what to do. They held their noses, and Sunaree told him, "Go in dat canal and wash off." She warned, "Now you hurry up and do dat. If you dont hurry up me and Rama goin to run and leff you!" Panday went inside the drain to clean himself. The water smelt of tadpoles. He looked into the water; there were hundreds of them; they were just playing and moving along with the current. He washed himself out quickly, then he joined Sunaree and Rama. Panday wanted to hold hands with them, but they refused. They were running again. They stopped suddenly. A streak of lightning ran down to the earth; it turned and twisted as a golden rope, then it lassooed a tree in the forest. It sounded *crash!!!*

Ma and Balraj came out of the sugarcane field. They went and sat under the long mango tree. The tree was very big, and it leaned over Tola Trace in a threatening way. The long mango tree was near Tola River; it was about halfway between the house and Rajput Road. Ma and Balraj sat as two heaps of straws. The mango tree was going *wish wish wish*, because the rain was beating the leaves. Ma had a deep cut in her forehead; she got it when Pa struck her by the rainwater barrel. As the water fell on her head, the blood mixed with the water on her eyelashes, the blood and the water formed a little ball, then the ball slipped gently down her nose; it stopped on the tip of her nose, then it fell *tuts* on her wet bosom. Ma felt her forehead with her hand. It was still bleeding.

"Bring some guava leafs son," she told Balraj.

"Yeh, Ma."

Balraj was cold all over, but he wanted to get the leaves. Ma was bleeding. He walked away from the long mango tree. The sky was dancing in blackness; clouds were running and piling up as a huge heap of black rice. Balraj got tender leaves from the very top of the guava tree. He walked back to the long mango tree with a handful. Ma was no longer under the tree. "Ay Ma!" he called fearfully.

"I on dis side of de tree," Ma said.

The long mango was bigger than any house in Tola. It was taller than a carat tree. The trunk was thick and heavy. Ma was sitting on the western side, leaning against the bark. Balraj came and handed her the leaves, then he sat down next to her.

Ma held the leaves in her right palm. She spat on them. Then she crushed them between her slender palms. A greenish juice leaked out from her palms and fell on the ground. The juice smelt as something to eat. Ma looked at her right palm; the leaves were ground enough; it looked as if moss was growing in her palms. She gathered the green spots together with her left index fingers; she joined the spots up and made something like a green worm, then she lifted up her hand slowly as if the crushed leaves were heavier than a stone. *Slap!* she slapped the green stuff on her forehead. Some of the green stuff went outside the cut. She took her fingers and ran them gently down her forehead. Then she loosed her orhni from her head. Her hair was black as a black fowl, and much longer than a leather belt. She held the silky headdress with both hands, then she ripped a piece off with her jaw teeth. She took the strip and dressed the wound. She took the orhni and tied up her head again.

The rain didn't care about Tola. Rain was pounding the earth. Ma and Balraj saw the drops; they looked like fat white worms invading the earth from above. God was trying to tie the earth and the sky with the rain drops. The whole of Tola was dark and dismal.

The wind didn't care about Tola. The wind was beating the rain and the rain was pounding the earth. There were no lights in the sky; all that Ma and Balraj saw were layers and layers of blackness and rage. The choking sound of the thunder came from the sky *zip zip zip crash doom doomm doomed!* Then the lightning moved as a gold cutlass and swiped an immortelle tree beyond the river.

Balraj twisted as a shadow with fright. He did his hands so, and his feet went so, and his lips shook as two dry leaves shaking in the wind. His teeth were hitting each other as dry bamboo twigs *toorot toorot tat tat toorot.* He breathed *hoosh hash hoosh hash* as a carpenter's saw.

Ma sat with her back resting against the heavy mango trunk. She sat just as a piece of old cloth rammed into the corner of two tapia walls. The water ran down the mango trunk and fell on her back *clat clat clat*, then it ran behind her back and the tree and fell inside the drain.

When the lightning struck the tree in Tola Forest, Sunaree, Rama and Panday stood up like pillars in the trace; they were afraid; their hearts were beating *dub! dub! dub!* They tried to see the forest, but they barely made out the long mango tree. The rain was falling as if God was cleaning out the sky with water and rage. They stood together and prayed, but the rain drops touched their skins as needles, and they felt fear and pain covering them up. It was painful, but they had to move on. They were still running south along Tola Trace; they ran until they reached the long mango tree. Ma saw them.

Ma was shocked. She thought all the time that they were safe inside the house, safe from the wind and the rain, safe from Pa too. Ma called out, "Where all you goin chirens?"

Sunaree and Panday ran under the tree. Rama stood on the trace and watched the mango tree fearfully. "I not goin under dat tree," he said. "Dat mango tree leanin over de trace. I fraid it fall on top me."

"It not goin to fall," Ma said.

"But it leanin over de trace."

Ma had a hard time proving to Rama that he was going to be safe under the mango tree. She argued that the lightning was not going to come under the tree, because God was guiding the lightning through the darkness and the rain with his bright eyes. Rama still didn't believe that; he just stood by the drain and watched Ma with fear and doubt in his eyes.

Ma got up. She held Rama's hand and brought him under the long mango tree. She made him sit on top of Balraj;

Balraj didn't like the idea of Rama sitting on his lap, but he didn't say anything. Sunaree and Panday sat on the ground. Ma tried to shelter them from the wind and the rain. She placed her hands against the rough bark as if she was holding up the tree. But Ma was a fool. The wind didn't care and the rain didn't care. Ma was not a banana leaf; she was not strong as iron; she was not as fat as a ricebag; she was thinner than a burnt sugarcane and her hands were thinner than cutlass wire. Large black ants began climbing down the tree. One stung Ma in her right hand.

"All you chirens move from by de tree!"

Balraj, Sunaree, Rama and Panday moved from under the tree. They stood on Tola Trace and looked at Ma.

Ma stood under the tree and thought of something. She crossed the small drain too, and stood on Tola Trace. She told Balraj and Sunaree to cross the river, walk the quarter mile to Rajput Road and call Nanna and Nanny.

"But sappose we cant cross de river?" Sunaree asked.

Ma thought a little, then she said, "If de river high up den all you coud come back."

Balraj and Sunaree left.

Rama and Panday stood on the trace. They asked Ma to take them home, because they were feeling cold. Ma said they had to wait. Pa was home. Drunk. She had to wait for Nanna and Nanny to come, because Pa was worst than a snake.

Ma faced the wind and the rain as a thin living stump, but she was using her brain. Rama and Panday couldn't hear her brain working, because it worked as a seed growing. Ma stood with her hands over her face as if she was trying to see behind her red eyeballs. Then she removed her hands and told them, "I go carry all you in dat cane field."

Rama and Panday looked at the sugarcane field. The long leaves went *ssh ssh ssh*. They told Ma that they were afraid of the long black scorpions, because one time Nanny told them a story about a child who was eaten by scorpions in Rajput Road.

"But all you goin to be warm inside dat cane field."

They wanted to be warm, so they followed Ma.

Rain poured and poured over Tola. Little flashes of lightning moved as brass earrings and gold fishes in the sky. Rama and Panday walked behind Ma. They felt the sugarcane leaves bruising them; the prickles from the green leaves held on to their skins. It pained as if red ants were biting them. The ground under their feet was damp. There were layers and layers of damp and rottening cane straws on the ground. They felt their toes sinking into the straws as if they were sinking into heaps of vomit; just sinking and sinking and sinking.

"Stand up!" Ma told them.

They stood and waited.

Ma started to strip some leaves off the tall sugarcanes. Each time she stripped the leaves, it went *trash trash one two trash trash*. Ma got enough straws. She gathered them and made a bed upon the wet earth for Rama and Panday. Then she held the canes from two rows and tied the tops together. The cane tops formed a shelter over the bed of straws. "Now all you chirens rest on dem straws now."

Rama and Panday couldn't help getting on. They were naked and uncomfortable on the wet straws; they were cold and the straws were cold also. But rain was not wetting them; they heard the rain drops *tarat tat tarat tat tat*, but they were safe from the rain. Yet they couldn't rest; especially Rama; he was coughing worst than a dog. Dampness rose up from the earth and touched their bodies as dead fingers. The earth breathed, but they were restless.

Hours had passed. The rain was not falling heavy now, it was only drizzling. Ma heard the *klips klips tix tix* of the insects, and the *craw craw craw* of the huge water birds that lived near the river. She knew that it was almost evening. She told Rama and Panday that she was going to take them home.

Rama and Panday came out of the cane field together with Ma. Ma didn't want to go home. She walked with them up Tola Trace a little, but when she almost reached the house, she hid in a guava patch. Rama and Panday walked into the house. Pa was not at home. They went inside and flung open the southern window. When Ma saw the opened window, she knew that Pa was away. She came out of the guava patch and went home too.

Rama and Panday were cold. Ma got some old clothes and wiped their skins quickly. Rama's skin was hot as a ricepot.

"You sick son?"

"Yeh," Rama said.

Ma got some coconut oil and rubbed down Rama and Panday. She went inside the bedroom to get some dry clothes for them; she couldn't find any. Rama and Panday had two pairs of pants and two merinos but Ma had washed them earlier in the day. She took two old floursacks out of the cardboard box; with the kitchen knife she made holes in the floursacks to fit their heads and hands. Then she helped them to put on the floursacks. She took out a flourbag sheet from an old box. She spread the sheets on some empty ricebags. Then she said, "All you chirens sleep on dese ricebags."

Ma heard the cattle going *moh umoh*. She knew that they were getting on because they were hungry. "Now Rama and Panday stay in dis house. I goin to change dem cattle."

"I fraid to stay in dis house," Panday said.

"Why?"

"I fraid a spirit come from de bush and hold me in dis house."

"It not have no spirit in dat bush."

"I still fraid," Panday declared.

She left them inside the house. She went by the lime tree and got the sledgehammer, threw the sledge over her right shoulder and walked behind the house to the riceland. The riceland bank was about one hundred yards long. It began on the eastern side of the house and ran to the end of the riceland, right under the doodoose mango tree. Ma looked for the bank. But there was no bank; the water made the place look like a brown sea.

Panday was afraid to sleep in the house: Rama was groaning and getting on. He was bawling as if something was beating him or standing on his chest, he was just going *uh! uh! uh!* trying to drive away the fever like. Then Rama fell asleep like a dead dog. But although he was asleep, Rama was still making noise; he was breathing like this *choot choot scroosh scroosh* as when a fowl scratches the ground for a worm.

Panday was afraid. He was not afraid that Rama was going to die in the house so much; he was afraid that an evil spirit was going to kill him; one of those headless jumbies that lived on the silkcotton trees in the forest; the spirit was going into the house and eat Rama, then it was going to eat Panday too. He rested on the ricebags in fear, just waiting for the spirit to come into the house. But no spirit came. Panday stretched his hands and felt Rama's chest. It was hot. A dark fear came over him. He got up and ran outside, bawling "Ay Ma!"

Ma was changing the white cow; she was tethering the cow under the doodoose mango tree, because Pa never built a pen for the animals. Ma looked. Panday was standing in the yard and calling her real hard.

"Go back in dat house!"

"I fraid a spirit eat me!" Panday shouted.

"Go back in dat house boy!"

"I not goin. I fraid!"

Ma was watching Panday. But he had no intentions of going back into the house. Ma took the iron pickets and put them under the carat tree. She washed her hands in a drain and headed for home. When she reached the yard she asked Panday, "Wot you doin in dis yard?"

"I was fraidin in dat house."

"Boy it gettin night. Go back in dat house."

"Rama makin noise like a dead dog in dat house!"

And Ma: "Now dead dog dont make no noise. You hear me? Now you go in dat house and stay wid you bredder. You better go fast because if you fadder come home and meet you in dis yard, he goin to kill you wid lix. Now you be a good chile and go back in dat house."

Panday went back into the house.

Ma took the sledgehammer, walked past the rainwater barrel and put it under the lime tree. She washed her feet in a drain by the outhouse and went to see about Rama and Panday. As she entered the doorway, Panday said, "Ma I tell you he dead like a dog. Rama done dead. But it good he dead, now he cant pee on me in de night no more."

And Ma: "Now you hush dat mout Panday. You bredder not dead. He just sleepin. Rama have fever. Some lime tea go cut dat fever. Now you keep dat mout shut and let you bredder sleep."

"Oright."

Ma didn't change her clothes. The dress was wet and it clung to her body as if it was trying to eat her bones. She went into the backyard, got some lime leaves and went into the kitchen with them. She rested the leaves on the earthen floor, because there was no table in the kitchen. Then she went into the little shed on the southern side of the kitchen to get some coconut shells. There were some dry ones in the middle of the heap, but Ma had to be careful because many scorpions lived in the shed among the shells. She brought about ten shells back to the kitchen, placed five into the fireside, poured some kerosene upon them and started a fire.

Ma made the tea. Then she took two cups inside the house. "Chirens!"

"Yeh," Panday answered.

"Wake up Rama. I want all you to drink dis tea while it hot."

Rama was sleeping real strong. Panday shook him hard, saying, "Get up boy and drink dis tea befo you dead like a dog."

"Now you stop talkin like dat Panday," Ma said. "Notten wrong wid you bredder. He just have a little fever."

"Oright."

Panday shook Rama again. Rama opened his eyes and said, "I sick."

"Drink some lime tea son. It good for dat fever."

"I not want dat tea," Rama told her.

It was darkish inside the house. Ma went in the kitchen and got a flambeau. She held the light in one hand and the tea in the other. "God does see de trobble I does see in dis house. Boy drink dis tea and let you modder have a chance to rest she head in dis life."

"But Rama body hot like hell," Panday informed her.

Ma placed the tea on the ground. She felt Rama's body. He was hot and trembling. The fever was strong. Then Ma shook her head. "It is time Balraj and Sunaree come back from Rajput Road now. So long dey gone."

Balraj and Sunaree crossed the river and walked to Rajput Road. They stood at the end of Tola Trace and called: "Nanny!"

Nanny was inside the house beating the drum. She couldn't hear them, because she was sitting on an old bag and beating the drum very hard.

Balraj and Sunaree called many times, but there were no replies. They walked into the yard and called again. There was still no answer, so they walked up to the bamboo door. Balraj pushed open the door and walked inside the house.

"Ah!" Nanny bawled. Then she said, "All you make me fraid like hell."

Nanny pushed the hand drum aside. "Wot make all you chirens come by me house in dis rain?"

And Balraj started to talk as if rain was falling; talking and talking and telling Nanny how Pa came home and beated him and beated Ma too; telling her how Ma was in the cane field with Rama and Panday; telling her and telling her how Pa was a nasty man; nasty like a snake. Nanny listened. She listened to him; she did not try to stop him; she didn't even ask him to explain anything; she just listened and listened. Then Balraj stopped talking and Nanny started up; she said how Pa was a bad man from morning; how he was a snake and a drunkard. Then she said how Ma was a good woman, but Ma was too stupid. And so Nanny talked and talked and talked until she had nothing more to say.

There was a long silence, then Sunaree said, "Wen Nanna comin from work Nanny?"

"He comin late."

"Well we goin back home."

Nanny didn't want them to go, so she said, "Now all you change dem wet clothes. If all you wear dem wet clothes all you goin to get sick."

Nanny went into the bedroom and brought some dry clothes for them. She gave Sunaree a long cotton dress. It was too long for her, because Nanny was a tall skinny woman.

Sunaree took a piece of cord and tied it around her waist. Balraj changed into one of Nanna's old pants and a loose khaki shirt. He pulled the leather belt around his waist and asked, "How I lookin Nanny?"

"You lookin good."

Nanny dished out some food: dal, rice and coconut chutnee on sohari leaves. They ate.

When Balraj and Sunaree finished eating, Nanny gave them water to wash their hands. She took the sohari leaves and flung them in the rain. Then Nanny gave Sunaree a bamboo flute. Balraj sat and listened as she played the flute. Then Nanny took the brown hand drum and beated and beated until Nanna came from work.

The rain was over but the sky was still cloudy. It was getting dark inside the house. Nanny lighted a flambeau. Nanna was eating; he looked sadder than a poor-me-one. He chewed his food *scroosh scroosh*; he stopped and thought a little, then he chewed *scroosh scroosh* again.

"Me dorta shouda leff dat man," Nanny said. "She seein too much trobble wid him."

And Nanna: "Is one dorta I have in dis world. It have no peace for she. It better if she dead."

Nanna couldn't eat any more. He pushed the food away and stared at the light.

"You have no right to worry youself oldman. We near we grave now. A few more years and we goin to dead and pass out."

But Nanna said nothing. He just stared at the light.

It was pitch dark when Nanna, Nanny, Balraj and Sunaree left Rajput Road to walk the half mile up Tola Trace to the house. Nanna walked in front. With the drum tied around her neck, Nanny walked behind him. Sunaree held the bamboo flute in her hand as she walked almost abreast of Nanny.

Balraj walked behind. The ground was very slippery, they had to be careful.

When they reached Tola River, the water bawled as an evil spirit. The place was dark and the river was making noise, going *burp burp burp*. Nanna told them to wait. He walked alone to the river. The water was pushing hard. Water was already above the bamboo crossing. Nanna walked back to them *splunk splunk*. He took Balraj on his shoulder. Balraj was scared as a rat. With Balraj on his shoulder, Nanna made the crossing. He left Balraj under the long mango tree and came back for Sunaree. She sat on his shoulder. Then Nanna turned to Nanny and said, "You walk behine."

"Oright."

Sunaree was trembling. Nanna held her tight. He tested every footstep. The water reached over his knees at the middle of the crossing. Nanna was breathing *foo foo foo* like a bull. When they made the crossing, Nanna said "Praise God."

III

AUGUST WAS rice-planting month. The riceland was covered with water. It looked like a sea. Panday was scrubbing the pots with the coconut fibre. Ma was inside the house attending to Rama. She heard Panday scrubbing the pots in the kitchen, because the kitchen and the house were under the same roof. Only a tapia wall separated the bedroom from the kitchen. Ma covered Rama up with old bags. His nose was stuffed up. She took an old rag and cleaned it. "How you feelin son?"

"Me chest lightin up like fire."

"It hurtin you plenty?"

"Not plenty plenty," he replied. "But it hurtin like hell."

Ma didn't know what to do. She had tried almost everything: lime juice, lime tea, coconut oil and hot milk, but nothing seemed to work for Rama. Ma looked at his eyes; they were dark and sad and red. Rama was feeling cold and sick, but it was hard for Ma to do anything more for him.

"Panday!"

"Yeh Ma!"

"Come in dis house right now!"

"Why?"

"Boy you just come in dis house!"

"Oright!" he said as he walked out of the kitchen.

Ma sat on the earthen floor. She took Rama's head and placed it on her lap. Then she took some coconut oil and rubbed his head. "How you feelin son?"

"I sick. Feelin more sick."

Panday came inside the bedroom.

"You bredder sick bad," Ma said. "Balraj and Sunaree not home yet. Stay wid Rama in dis house. I goin by dat rumshop to see wot you fadder doin."

Panday stared at the flambeau in the bedroom and said that he was not going to stay in the house with Rama, because he was afraid of the evil spirits that lived in the forest.

"Well den go back and do dem pots."

"Oright."

Panday went back into the kitchen to wash the pots.

Then Ma put back Rama's head on the ricebag. She stood up and said, "Now you sleep Rama."

Ma walked out of the bedroom and came into the kitchen. Panday was still scrubbing away with the coconut fibre. Ma took the fibre from him, handed him a cocoyea broom, saying, "You sweep out de kitchen Panday."

The place was almost completely dark, but the wind was blowing easy easy. Now and then some pieces of lightning danced around the kitchen, but there was no thunder. The flambeau made the kitchen look alive. But the kitchen was very uncomfortable; the earthen floor was wet and cold. Panday held the thick coconut broom in both hands, bending down to sweep as if he was a cripple. When he was almost finished, he bawled out, "Looka skopian!"

Ma took the iron pot from the other side of the kitchen and ran by Panday. "Where de skopian?" she asked.

Panday told her he had seen a large black scorpion on the earthen floor. When he called her, the scorpion had crawled back into a crack in the wall.

"You sure you see a skopian boy?"

"Yeh Ma. I see a skopian."

"Well put down dat broom," Ma said. "Go in dat house and sleep wid Rama."

"Oright."

It was dark. Night came early like. Black clouds were moving up and down in the sky. The thunder began a slow grumble as if it was pulling itself away from the forest and the sky, then it began to shake up Tola. Ma knew that it was going to rain again. She was worried. She heard something. She listened.

A drum was beating. It kept on beating. Well. It kept on beating and beating and beating and beating. . . . The rain began to drizzle. Ma heard the rain drizzling. Then the rain came down real hard and the lightning danced and the thunder shook up Tola. Then the wind came out from the sky and began to pull the trees and shake the house. But the drum was still beating. She held the flambeau in her hand. The wind was trying to out the light. When the drumming almost reached the house, Ma called, "Ay!"

"Oy!" Nanny answered.

Ma was happy. She listened to the drum. It beated faster and faster. She heard the drum beating inside her chest. It was beating fast and hard and fast and hard; just beating inside her chest and in the sky.

Nanna, Nanny, Balraj and Sunaree walked inside the house. They were soaked all over as if they had fallen inside the river. The drum was tied around Nanny's neck; it was brown as a brown cow. Ma went out into the yard to meet them, then she carried them inside the kitchen. She took out rice and dal. They ate.

When the food was finished, they washed their hands with rainwater that fell from the thatched roof. The water felt like ice. Balraj was trying to wash his whole hand. He leaned over; almost over the drain. There was a flash of lightning the same time. He jumped up and fell down inside the canal. Nanna and Nanny rushed into the drain and took him out. They carried him to the rainwater barrel. He had a good bath at the back of the house. They brought him into the kitchen.

"How Rama feelin?" Nanny asked Ma.

"He sick wid fever."

"He sick bad?"

"Me eh know," Ma said. "But all you coud go and see him inside. He sleepin wid Panday."

Nanna and Nanny went into the bedroom to see Rama. He was asleep, but he was breathing hard hard. Panday was asleep too. They walked back to the kitchen, and Nanny said to Ma, "Rama have bad fever."

And Ma: "Me husban in de rumshop. He not care notten about dese chirens. But by de grace of God dese same chirens goin to come man and woman in dis same Tola."

"But Rama have to see a docta," Nanny said.

And Nanna put on a worried look. "I goin by dat rumshop to see me son-in-law. He have to come home and help me say some prayers for dis chile."

"Oright," Nanny said.

Nanna walked out of the kitchen into the drizzle and the night.

About an hour after Nanna left, Nanny started to beat the drum. The rain was falling making its own music. Sunaree was playing the flute. Nanny's fingers were long and bony. They touched the goat's skin as if they were accustomed to it. She beated the drum slow slow. Sunaree played the flute good; her fingers touched the holes in the bamboo flute as if they were made for them. The music of the flute was sweeter than sugar; than life even. Ma was dancing. Balraj was watching. The kitchen was full of music and sadness: music from the sky and the earth, but sadness from the earth alone. And their spirits were growing and floating in the air like silkcotton flowers.

Nanny started a song. Her eyes were dark and sad. She sang a part and Ma repeated it. Ma sang a line, and she repeated it. So it went on and on. The song was in Hindi. The sky God was listening, because the drum was beating like cake over Tola; like honey. It was beating and beating and beating; beating only to keep them awake like bats; it was beating only to keep them happy and sad, happy and sad; it was beating for the black night that was choking Tola, and the rain that was pounding the earth; the drum was beating in the sky and it was beating on the earth; it was beating, and even the great sky God could not stop it from beating, because it was beating and beating and beating just as the heavens roll.

Suddenly it ended. Nanny said to Ma, "You have good chirens. God go help dem one day. Wid all dis blackness choking Tola from all sides, it hard for dem later on."

"God go help dem," Ma said with great sadness in her voice.

Nanny beated the drum again. This time she beated for the tadpoles, the scorpions and the night birds; she beated not only for the living things of Tola; she beated a tune for all that lives and moves upon the face of the earth. She beated and she knew that the great sky God was watching with his big big eyes.

A large cockroach with long wings flew *flut* over the light. It settled *taps* on the earthen wall. It was wet; it came from the rain to shelter near the light. Nanny took the brown hand drum and crushed it *crachak!* Then Sunaree took the flute and crushed it; crushed it to nothingness.

The rain continued to fall. Fall really heavy, as if the rice-land was going to overflow and cover the whole house. Ma, Nanny, Balraj and Sunaree stood inside the kitchen. White sprays jumped over the wall and soaked them. The wind was strong; it was as if big big winds were leaving from far away and blowing over Tola and the whole of the island; blowing with such force and temper; blowing with the intention of crippling even the trees, blowing just to cause trouble and hate. Ma kept lighting the flambeau. Each time she did, the strange winds outed it. Rain began to fall through the holes in the roof, soaking their heads. Some of the needle grass was blown off the roof by the wind. Rain poured through the holes more and more. Inside the kitchen, the floor was getting slippery; almost too slippery to stand. There were small holes in the earthen floor. They were filling up with water. Ma kept lighting the flambeau; it was no use.

"Like Pa send dat wind," Balraj said.

"De wind and de rain too strong for de flambeau," Nanny said.

They couldn't stand any more, so they squatted. Nanny held the drum in her lap. Cold water from the rottening rafters kept falling on their heads. Falling and running down their faces. There were crickets too inside the kitchen; by the tens, jumping crazily. Balraj and Sunaree were afraid of them. Ma pulled out a strip of tarpaulin from behind the machan, it was cold, with holes all over; but it smelt like something to eat. She gave it to Balraj and Sunaree to cover their heads. Now the water was flowing on the earthen floor; just flowing as a river flows. It was getting colder and colder.

"Ay Ma!" Panday screamed from inside the house.

Ma and Nanny ran inside the house. Water was seeping through the needle grass on the roof and wetting Rama. Ma and Nanny grabbed the ricebags and skidded them along the earthen floor. They looked up. The roof was leaking in many places.

"Rama sick. He cant get wet. Wot we goin to do?" Ma asked.

"Put Rama inside de ricebox," Nanny advised.

Balraj and Sunaree were in the bedroom helping Ma and Nanny out.

"All you help put Rama in dat ricebox," Ma said.

"Oright," Balraj replied.

Ma and Nanny grabbed one side of the ricebags; Balraj, Sunaree and Panday held the other end. They carried Rama out of the bedroom. Rama was crying, so they rested him down near the bedroom door. Then they picked him up again and carried him by the ricebox.

There was no time to ask Rama why he was crying. The roof was leaking more and more. They had to put Rama inside the ricebox quickly, because he was sick. Ma said to Balraj, "Open dat ricebox fast. We have to put Rama in dat box right now."

"Oright."

The ricebox was six feet long and four feet wide. Balraj opened the lid. He went inside. Ma held the light over the box. The unground rice in the box was wet; Balraj levelled it out with his hands. When the box was prepared, he came out.

They lifted Rama slowly; they lifted him as if he was dead. Balraj climbed back into the box. He took the light from Ma and placed it inside the box. With the flambeau inside it, the ricebox looked like a big rottening pumpkin. Then Balraj climbed out of the box. Rama and the light were shut into the box.

"I feelin cold," Panday said.

The rain sang and the thunder shouted and the lightning danced.

Ma picked up Panday. Her back was resting against the wall. She stared at the light inside the box, trying to see Rama. Nanny made a step forward. She slipped. She was falling with her head over the drum. Nanny prevented the fall by grabbing hold of the wall. The rain was falling heavier now. Brown water almost covered the floor. Outside, the thunder and the rain were shouting at Tola, and the sky God was listening; listening real good. Ma and Nanny began to speak in Hindi. Balraj, Sunaree and Panday couldn't understand too well, but they knew what Ma and Nanny were talking about: they were talking about the rain and life; the rain and the thunder; the rain and the wind; the rain and the darkness; the rain and the past, and about the rain and the future; and about life and death.

There were small cracks in the earthen wall. Red ants started to come out of the cracks. First a few, then many. They started to sting. Real hard. It was as if fire was burning their skins. They moved from against the wall, but the ants were still stinging them, ants were in their clothes and their hair. They leaned against the ricebox; against the cold cedar board. Sunaree got a scrape in her back with a nail. She started to cry.

Rama was coughing and crying inside the ricebox; crying and coughing as if he was going to die. The water from the roof was still falling upon the box.

"Balraj!"

"Yeh Ma."

"Son take de cutlass from de kichen. Go cut some fig leafs and bring dem and cover de roof. Rama feelin cold. He not sappose to get wet all de time."

"Oright."

The place was dark. Balraj went in the kitchen and got the cutlass. He went by the banana patch to the southern side of the house. He couldn't see to cross the drain. He waited for the lightning; as it flashed, he jumped over the drain. Balraj felt the wet leaves with one hand and he chopped them off the banana trunk with the other.

When he came back with the leaves, he saw that they were

badly torn by the wind. He handed them to Ma and Nanny, and went back for some more. Ma and Nanny held the leaves over their heads. Crickets were jumping all over the place. Sunaree and Panday kept rubbing their feet against each other, trying to kill the crickets like.

Rama was crying and getting on inside the box; he was saying how he was getting wet.

The light was shut inside the box, because when Balraj had closed the lid, he closed the light in. Ma gave her leaves to Nanny. She went into the kitchen and made another flambeau. She came back and handed the light to Nanny. It was as if Ma didn't want to have anything to do with the light.

Balraj brought the banana leaves. This time he was more careful; they were not torn by the wind. Balraj handed the leaves to Ma. He climbed up on the ricebox. He stood on the lid, and Ma handed him the leaves. He began to push the leaves between the rafters and the needle grass. But he couldn't fit the leaves properly, because the roof was too high. Nanny got a potato crate and handed it to Balraj. He took it and placed it on top of the ricebox. He stood on the crate in order to reach the roof easily. Balraj was working real fast. The water began to fall on the ricebox less and less. He was trying hard to cover the roof, but . . .

"O God!" he shouted.

Balraj jumped down from the ricebox. He fell on the ground and started to scream, bawling as if the life was coming out of him, getting on as if he was quarrelling with the wind and the rain. Ma and Nanny thought he saw an evil spirit; they began talking in Hindi right away, saying prayers and this kind of thing. Balraj was rolling in the water, keeping his hands high in the air. The rain was pouring and pouring and pouring down on Tola. Lightning flashed. Balraj told Ma and Nanny that his hands were on fire. The water came

down from the roof and fell on the ricebox *drip drip drip*.
Something fell from the roof *tats*; it fell harder than the water.

Ma and Nanny moved closer to the ricebox with the
flambeau. There were three of them. Full grown. Deadly.
Moving fast. Faster. Running on the ricebox. They were black
like rubber. The long legs were hurrying. Tails in the air. Moving faster and faster. Fire stingers. The scorpions. Little but
deadly; they kept running and running.

"Move fast!" Ma shouted.

Sunaree shifted.

The scorpions were running down the sides of the ricebox.
Nanny crushed one with the drum. Ma burnt another with
the flambeau; it smelt bad. Some more fell on the ricebox. The
scorpions were running down the sides of the box too fast.
They couldn't kill all of them. Ma took the flambeau and
started to smoke them off the ricebox. She didn't want them
to go inside the box, because Rama was still inside the box.
And the scorpions were running crazily all over the place; just
running with their tails in the air. Some of them went underneath the box. Others just crawled on the earth in the muddy
water. Some went into the cracks of the earthen wall. A large
black scorpion was climbing on Sunaree's right foot. She
jumped up, and it fell in the water again. She took the flute
and pounded it to death; pounded it just as the rain was
pounding the house, and the wind was pounding the light.

Balraj was still bawling and rolling in the water. Rama too
was screaming from inside the ricebox; screaming and saying
how the scorpions were stinging him.

Nanna reached same time.

IV

NANNA RAN *splunk splunk* into the house. Balraj was rolling in the water. He was bawling. Nanna had no time with Balraj; he just jumped over him and ran by the ricebox.

Nanna didn't say a word. He ran by the box. The light that Balraj had placed inside the ricebox was out, so Rama was in darkness. Water still fell from the roof on the ricebox. Nanna stretched his skinny hands and lifted the ricebox cover. The cover was heavy, and Nanna was an old man, but he just pulled the cover like nothing and opened the box.

"Show me de light," he said.

Nanny leaned over the opened ricebox with the flambeau. Nanna saw two scorpions inside the box. "Hand me someting fast!" he shouted, as he climbed into the box.

Nanny handed him the drum. The scorpions were making a run for it. But they couldn't run from the drum. Nanna held the drum firmly, and pounded them *bup bup bup*.

Rama was bawling, and the wind and the rain were shouting at Tola and pounding the earth; water came through the holes in the roof more and more. Nanna picked up Rama. He handed him to Nanny and Ma. Nanna took the drum and came out of the box; the scorpions couldn't interfere with him, because he had the drum.

Balraj was rolling in the water; he was twelve years old, yet he was rolling in the water. The whole house was spinning with noise and water. Nanna picked up Balraj. "Now hush!"

"I deadin. Fire lightin in me hand."

Nanna told Sunaree and Panday to get some ricebags and spread them out by the tapia wall. Sunaree and Panday went into the bedroom. It was dark. They felt the ground, slippery and cold under their feet. They searched with their toes for the empty ricebags. They were searching quietly because they were afraid that an evil spirit was going to hold them in the bedroom.

"I get one bag," Panday said.

He bent down and took up the bag.

"Now shake out dat bag good, befo a skopian bite you," Sunaree warned.

"Oright."

Panday shook the bag *vat vat vat* in the darkness. It sounded as if he was opening a dry coconut with a dull cutlass.

Sunaree got a few bags too. She shook them and said to Panday, "Let we come outa dis dark place. I fraid if a lightnin cut out we tongues."

"Why you makin me fraid?"

"I not makin you fraid."

Nanna heard them arguing, so he said, "Come fast wid dem bags."

"Oright," Sunaree answered.

When they brought the bags, Nanna said, "Spread dem bags by dat tapia wall. It not have no skopians dere."

Nanna placed Balraj upon the bags. Nanny and Ma rested Rama next to Balraj.

"It not have no dry coverlets for dese chirens to put under dey backs?" Nanna asked.

"No," Ma said sadly.

And Nanny: "Me God! Where you is God!"

Nanna picked up a dead scorpion from the water. It was long and black. He took the light from Nanny and began

41

roasting it. The scorpion went *sooey soeey*, then *crack crack crack*, as the flame licked the flesh. It smelt as if rubber or wet leaves were burning. The smoke came out bluish like. Then he removed the body from the flame; he blew it, then he broke out the end of the tail and threw it away. Then with a slow patience he roasted the body of the scorpion again. Nanna took the roasted scorpion and came near Balraj and Rama.

"Eat dis," Nanna said, handing Balraj a piece of roasted scorpion. "It go do you good."

"I not want dat!"

"Eat it boy. It good for you."

"Me eh want it, I say."

Nanna reminded Balraj that he and Rama were stung by deadly scorpions; the poison was working fast; they were going to die if they didn't eat the roasted scorpion.

"Sappose we eat it and still dead?" Balraj asked.

"Never!" Nanna replied.

Resting on the wet bags, Balraj and Rama ate the scorpion meat. They ate in fear, because their eyes were wide open as doors. When they finished the meat, Nanna made his hands into a cup. He asked Balraj and Rama to piss in his hands. Rama coughed and said that he was too sick to piss. Balraj kept saying that his bladder was empty, because he had pissed when he went for the banana leaves.

Sunaree and Panday were listening. They were looking on; feeling sorry for Balraj and Rama like.

"I go pee in you hand Nanna," Panday said.

Nanna objected. He said that the piss was going to act against the poison only if it came from Balraj and Rama.

"Now Balraj and Rama all you pee in me hand!"

"I not!" Balraj said.

"Well den you goin to dead! And Rama too!" Nanna shouted.

When Balraj learnt that if he and Rama didn't pass water they were going to die, he began to piss in a great hurry. Nanna took the piss and rubbed it on Balraj's hands; on his face; some even went into his mouth. Balraj spat; "Man Nanna, pee does taste wost dan skopian meat I tell you!"

With Balraj it was easy, but Nanna had a great deal of trouble with Rama. His feet were trembling; he was almost too weak to stand, but he was strong enough to piss.

Then Balraj and Rama settled on the wet ricebags again. Balraj was silent, but Rama was going *kohok! kohok! kohok!* like a dog.

Nanna looked on with worried eyes. He believed that some evil spirit was causing Rama to cough like a dog; the evil spirit was making the poison work too. Nanna started to recite some mantras from the Hindu scriptures; he was trying his best to drive away the evil spirit. But the spirit was upon Rama alone, because Balraj was not coughing like a dog; only Rama was coughing like a dog and getting on. Nanna stopped, then he told Nanny and Ma to go and get some scorpion bush.

Nanny took a cutlass, and Ma held a flambeau; they went behind the house to look for the bush. The rain was still falling. They saw the night bolted against the sky; they witnessed the total darkness rebelling against the light and life; the night loomed and loomed and loomed as a mountain of wet coals before them. They heard the wind ripping Tola as a claw from the shapeless darkness; there was the thunder too, reaching through the night as a potent god to clout them. In the darkness they felt the fear pinching their hearts.

"Careful de drain," Nanny said.

Nanny spoke too late. Ma fell *splash!* inside the drain. Nanny helped her up. They walked on.

Water came from the riceland and covered up most of the yard. Most of the scorpion bush was covered by water.

"All dis trobble," Ma said, "and me husban not know not-ten. He by some rumshop drinkin rum. But by de help of God, me chirens goin to come man and woman in Tola."

"Stupidness! Leff de man."

Ma said she was not going to leave Pa. She was prepared to stick with him somehow.

"Dat is because you stupid," Nanny said.

Ma and Nanny kept on looking. They heard the frogs croaking in the yard, and they heard the night birds beyond the river going *craw*.

Sunaree and Panday took out their eyes when Nanna said that an evil spirit was causing Rama to cough like a dog; they were afraid of the evil spirits, especially the ones who didn't like children. They believed that the spirit came from the forest because of the rain; the spirit was really strong on Rama, because the rain was falling and falling and making the spirit mad. Sunaree and Panday stood close to Nanna and looked on.

Nanna closed his eyes as he recited the Sanskrit verses; he was begging the great sky God and also the minor Aryan gods; he was begging the gods; begging them to forsake their beds and their wives in heaven; begging them just to look down from the sky through the rain clouds on Balraj and Rama. He was talking to the gods like a child. He was asking them to drive away the darkness and the rain and beat the evil spirit out of the house. He believed the gods were listening to him. He opened his eyes and blew three times on Balraj. He closed his eyes again, disturbed the gods again, blew three times on Rama too, then he closed his eyes again. . . . Suddenly he asked Balraj, "How you feelin?"

"I still sick."

Just as Nanna was about to pray again, Nanny and Ma

walked into the house with the scorpion bush. Nanny handed him the bush saying, "We had to look like hell for dem bush."

"We go use de bush later," Nanna said.

"Why?" Ma asked.

"Because de prayers have to work."

Nanna stood up. He closed his eyes tight, and started to pray hard hard; he was not quarrelling with God or anything; he was just begging him to beat the evil spirit and drive away the rain. Nanna prayed and prayed and prayed, but God was too busy sending the rain to drown the earth.

"Stop prayin!" Nanny shouted.

But Nanna closed his eyes even tighter and prayed more and more.

Nanny pushed him and said, "Stop prayin you modderass! De chirens sick. Give dem de skopian bush."

Nanna opened his eyes and said that the prayers were going to work, because the Aryan gods were willing to help.

"Look! Give de chirens de medicine!"

"Oright!" Nanna shouted.

Nanna bent down, picked up the leaves and went into the kitchen. He washed them out with the rainwater that fell from the thatched roof. Then he took the rolling pin and ground the leaves. When he was satisfied, he threw the leaves into a lota, then he poured some water into the brassware and stirred the water with his fingers. He tasted the mixture. It was bitterish, but good. He walked out of the kitchen with the bush medicine.

"Drink half Balraj and leff half for Rama," Nanna directed.

Balraj drank half of the medicine and gave the lota to Rama; Balraj didn't make a bad face or anything like that; he just handed the lota to Rama, wiped his mouth with the rice-bag, and remained quiet as a stone. But Rama didn't even bother to drink; he just handed Nanna the lota and lied down on the bags as a dead dog.

Rama was too sick; he couldn't even sit up properly. He was lying down on the ricebags without even bothering to groan.

"Rama feelin good," Nanna said. "He not even groanin. De prayers workin now."

"Give Rama some medicine!" Nanny shouted.

"But de prayers workin. If de prayers cant help no medicine cant help!"

"You just give dat chile dat medicine!"

Nanna grumbled, but he bent down, lifted Rama's head, and put the lota to his lips. Rama took a long time to drink; even so, he drank just a little. Then Nanna rested him on the ricebags again.

Nanny stood looking at Balraj and Rama. She felt sorry for them. She wanted them to sleep, because once they were asleep, they would have nothing to fear. Nanny unstrung the drum from around her neck. She sat on the slippery floor with her back resting against the tapia wall, then she beated the drum slowly. Nanny was a good drummer, the best in Tola. Her fingers moved slow and clever. Nanny swayed from side to side as if she was trying hard to make the drum talk. Ma and Sunaree danced. Panday listened. But Nanna was standing as a carat tree and praying hard like hell. Suddenly the drumming ended. Nanny stood up as a cane shoot. Rama was vomiting *orks sputs orks sputs.* . . . He was vomiting as if he was dying; vomiting green green on the ricebags.

"O God me chile deadin!" Ma screamed.

Ma ran and held on to Rama; he was still vomiting; his eyes were closed, but he was seeing, just as jumbie bird sees in daylight.

Nanna opened his eyes and said, "He not deadin. Have patience. God goin to drive dat spirit away."

And Nanny: "Stop prayin oldman! Go and get a horse cart and take dese chirens to Tolaville Haspital."

"I not goin," Nanna replied. "God have to drive dat spirit away!"

Nanny ran up to Nanna. She told him that he had to get the horse cart and carry Balraj and Rama to Tolaville Hospital, because the prayers were of no use.

"But de river too high up," Nanna cooed.

"To hell wid de river! Take dese chirens to de hospital else dey goin to dead in dis house."

Nanny was talking hard, but Nanna was talking easy. He said he needed a horse cart, but he reminded Nanny he had no horse cart. The hospital was three miles away; he couldn't carry them on his head. Tola River was high; even if he got a horse cart borrow in Rajput Road he couldn't cross Tola River with the cart to come to the house.

"Swim dat river and borrow a horse cart!" Nanny shouted.

Nanna explained that the river was going *burp burp* . . . the night birds were going *craw craw craw*. The night was turning and twisting like a black spider; and the thunder, the lightning and the rain were ripping up Tola as if the sky God was mad.

Nanny was in a rage; Rama was vomiting; Ma was bawling; and Balraj was getting on and getting on and getting on.

"Now you go and get dat horse cart!" Nanny screamed.

"But how I goin to cross dat river wid dat horse cart?" Nanna asked in a high voice.

Nanny told him to get a horse cart in Rajput Road, then go up to Atkinson Settlement, cross the iron bridge, then come to Tola Trace through Karan Settlement.

"But if I go all dat distance wid de horse, by de time I come back day goin to be clean out. Dat go take too long. Lemme pray a little more and see if it go help."

"Go! Go! Go!!!" Nanny screamed.

Nanna left same time.

Ma was bawling, "De poison cover up me chile!"

And Nanny: "Don't get on so! You is a big woman. Wen you get on so you makin de chirens fraid."

And Sunaree: "We done fraid like hell Nanny!"

Ma felt grief; her grief was not as shallow as a basket, it was deeper than a river; deep like the sea; like a sea without fishes.

"Bring some coconut oil Panday," Nanny said.

"I fraid like hell to go in dat kitchen Nanny. I fraid a jumbie hold me and eat me."

"Go wid him," Nanny said to Sunaree.

Sunaree walked in front. Panday followed her, but not too close because he was afraid of the jumbie. It was dark, but Sunaree knew exactly where to find the coconut oil.

"Wot God doin now?" Panday asked.

"He watchin from de sky."

"But de sky black like coals."

"God still watchin."

"Well God playin de ass now!"

Sunaree told Panday that God was going to make the Devil eat him *crips crips*. Panday ran out of the kitchen. Sunaree brought the coconut oil and handed it to Nanny. Nanny removed the brown paper cap. She took some oil and rubbed down Rama. Then Nanny moved over a little and rubbed down Balraj too.

"Dat trow up on dem bags smellin wost dan cow pee!" Panday said.

"God go bite you," Sunaree warned.

"All you shut all you mouts!" Ma shouted.

Nanny felt good. She felt just like a doctor. She put the oil bottle to Rama's lips and told him to drink. Rama drank. But he started to vomit again; he wasn't vomiting anything; just the coconut oil that went green in his stomach.

"God! Dis time me chile deadin!" Ma bawled.

Nanny trembled. "Hush! De chile go live. Just now de horse cart comin. Keep corage."

And Ma: "Me chile deadin!"

"Stop gettin on so!" Nanny shouted.

Ma listened to her. She stopped the bawling, but she couldn't remain quiet; she sobbed and sobbed and sobbed, and the tears just rolled down her face.

Nanny didn't know what to do. The rain was falling and the thunder and the lightning were walking all over the village; just walking all over the place. Nanny took the hand drum and beated and beated and beated until Nanna came.

"You get de horse cart?" Nanny asked doubtfully.

"Yeh," Nanna answered.

"Where it is?"

"Over de river."

"But how you goin to take Balraj and Rama over dat river?" Nanny asked.

Nanna explained how he couldn't go all the way to Atkinson Settlement with the horse; it was a waste of time. He just borrowed the cart from Rajput Road, came up Tola Trace, swam the river, and came to carry Balraj and Rama to Tolaville.

"But how you goin to carry dem over de river?"

"I go swim wid dem."

"But sappose dey drown?"

"Den I go drownd wid dem!"

There was no time to waste. Nanna took up Balraj and Nanny picked up Rama. They walked out of the house. Ma, Sunaree and Panday walked behind.

The sky rolled as an endless spider and the rain fell like a shower of poison over Tola. The darkness was thicker than black mud, and the wind howled as evil spirits.

Long before they reached the river, they heard the *hush hush hush* of the current; but they walked on. When they reached the river the water was high up.

Nanna took Balraj and swam the river; the current was pushing hard, but Nanna was a good swimmer. He made it. He called from the other side saying, "Balraj safe on de odder side now!"

"Oright!" Nanny shouted.

When Nanna came to collect Rama, he was tired. Blowing. He rested a little. While he rested, Nanny said, "Oldman take care of youself."

"I see enuff days in Tola. Me eh fraid to dead."

Nanna got up. He took Rama and went into the water. Nanny, Ma, Sunaree and Panday stood as a heap of living mud; just waiting for Nanna to cross safely. Then the time grew long; long like a rope, and tied them like a rope too. Their bodies formed one great beast reaching up to the sky. And the clouds opened and out of the middle came water; water that washed away the earth into the mouth of the darkness. Then the thunder beated as the heart of rage in space, and out of the space came the lightning as a great spike and it stabbed the mouth of darkness. And the winds became hot and carried death into all the corners . . . then the rope caught fire and the great beast danced to the tune of death between the darkness and the void. The beast danced even though it knew it was going to die . . . it danced and danced, till the void and the darkness strangled the beast . . .

"All you go home now!" Nanna shouted from the other side.

"Oright!" Nanny said.

Nanny, Ma, Sunaree and Panday hurried home through the rain.

V

Two days had passed. The rain was over, but the earth was wet and it smelt like new. The water in the riceland was low. Pa sat on a crate; he was eating a shard of roti. He wasn't drunk, but his eyes looked like dirt. Then he stopped chewing the roti. "Eat fast Sunaree and Panday. All you have to plant rice."

Ma stood near the ricebox. She didn't eat but her belly was full; full of worries. Her eyes were almost hidden in her bony sockets. She said to Pa, "Now you let dese chirens eat in peace. Balraj and Rama still in dat haspital. So you let dese chirens eat."

Pa sat on the crate. He went on eating, but he shook his feet all the time. Suddenly he threw his food away. "I go take a chila and beat all you modderass in dis house!"

He was waiting for Ma to say something. She said nothing. Pa walked out of the house.

Sunaree and Panday sat on the earthen floor. They ate fast, chewing like hell just to please Ma.

"Now all you take all you time," Ma said. "It not good to eat fast fast."

Sunaree and Panday couldn't reply to this; their mouths were full of food. They only shook their heads. Ma rested her hands on the tapia wall and looked at them. She didn't smile with them or anything; she just looked at them. They watched her too. Then Sunaree gulped down her food and said, "We is good chirens."

"Yeh," Ma said as she turned to go in the kitchen.

Panday chewed slowly. Sunaree told him to hurry up.

"I not hurryin up. I not plantin no rice today. I fraid dem snakes in dat wadder."

Ma came out of the kitchen. She had an old floursack tied around her head. She said that she was going in front to pull the rice nurseries; Sunaree and Panday were to come later.

"No Ma. Wait for me!" Panday said.

"Come wid Sunaree."

"I fraid a spirit eat me in dis house."

Ma laughed. Ugly. She had very few teeth in her mouth; they had fallen off long ago.

"Ma you ugly like a rat rat rat," Panday sang.

Ma didn't mind. She picked up Panday in her skinny arms. Panday started to cry. He didn't want Ma to hold him. He complained that if she fell, he was going to fall too. She put him down.

Ma walked in front as if she was walking a race or something. Sunaree and Panday walked behind. There were red crabs on the riceland bank. They moved away as Ma walked up to them. But some of them were fat and lazy; lazy just as fat people. Their bellies were big and they looked like red cashews. Sunaree and Panday tried their best to meet Ma. They couldn't. Ma was a fast walker, but she couldn't walk as fast as Jesus. Sunaree and Panday trailed behind. Then *chax!* Panday walked on a fat crab. Sunaree looked over her shoulder and said, "God goin to give you sin Panday!"

"But me eh do it for spite."

"You still goin to get sin."

"Me eh do it for spite I tellin you."

"Oright," Sunaree said, "but dat crab have plenty young ones in she belly. Now you kill dat crab and all dem young ones too."

Sunaree and Panday sat on the riceland bank and looked at the female crab. The crab's feet were still moving; trembling like. Something white as cow's milk flowed out of the crushed and upturned belly. Then the feet became dead.

"De crab dead now," Sunaree said sadly.

"God know it dead?"

"Yeh, God know dat."

Panday remained worried and quiet. Sunaree held the crab with her tiny fingers; part of the back was buried in the mud; the mud formed a dirty circle around the belly. She looked carefully; some of the young crabs were moving inside the broken shell. She lifted the dead crab and placed it gently in the water.

Ma was at the end of the riceland bank. She looked back; Sunaree and Panday were still sitting almost at the other end of the bank. "All you come on chirens, it gettin late!" Ma said.

They got up and ran to her.

Ma sat on a potato crate and pulled out the rice plants from the muddy water. The nurseries were thin and long, and softer than grass. Ma pulled them fast with her bony fingers.

Hundreds of brown doves kept flying over the riceland. Their wings went *tat tat tat tat tat* as if dry leaves were rubbing against each other. Black birds rose like a steady flow of smoke, passed over the riceland and settled on the long mango trees.

Sunaree wore a long dress made from a floursack. Panday was dressed in a merino only; he wasn't wearing any pants. They sat on the upturned crate near Ma, and helped her pull the rice plants out of the ground. Then Pa came into the water and joined them. He knew the work well, but he couldn't pull the plants out of the ground faster than Ma. But Pa didn't pull for long. He took a brushing-cutlass and started trimming the grass on the narrow meri. As he cutlassed some of the cut grass fell back into the water.

Several mango trees lined the northern edge of the rice-land. They were tall. Some of them had wild pines growing on their branches. Ripe mangoes fell inside the riceland; that made the water blackish near the trees. The water smelt bad too, because the mangoes were rottening inside of it.

"Come and take up dese grass!" Pa shouted.

Sunaree and Panday got up. They walked fast. Pa was cutlassing the grass on the bank. Sunaree and Panday took the grass that fell in the water, made them into small balls and placed them on the meri.

When they were finished picking up the grass, they went and joined Ma. It was time to scatter the rice nurseries. Ma held the tops of the rice plants and broke them off, because this made the plants grow better. Then she collected them into small handfuls, and tied them into small faggots. Sunaree and Panday threw the faggots out all over the riceland.

"Help me plant some rice," Ma said.

"No," Pa declared.

"Why?"

"Kiss me ass! Dat is why."

Ma remained quiet as a mango skin. She didn't even look at Pa. She took up a faggot of rice plants in her left hand, loosed the banana string that held it together and started to plant the rice. Ma was always a good planter. The plants stood upright, about eight inches above the water, because the roots were well buried under the water; the plants did not lean too much in any direction. She made a straight row along the bank; went a little way with it; then she turned around and made another row. The faggot planted about three rows. Then she took another one, and planted *chooks chooks chooks* again.

Sunaree and Panday planted too. Sunaree and Panday knew about rice planting, but Sunaree did most of the work. Panday spent his time looking for red crabs in the water.

Panday didn't want to kill the crabs; he felt sorry for crabs; he was only trying to get them out of Sunaree's way; he didn't want her to kill them by mistake. It was very hard to see the crabs in the water; it was too muddy. Panday just ran his hands in the water; whenever he found a crab, he caught it and threw it out of the way. He had to be careful because the red crabs had sharp gundies.

Sunaree planted slow, but she planted good. Once or twice she tried to move fast, but the plants didn't stand upright, because the roots were not placed in the ground firmly; they were uprooted by the wind.

Pa went under the doodoose mango tree. He sat down and ate mangoes all the time. He ate just like a pig; the yellow juice rolled down his face and fell on his chest, and hundreds of flies licked his lips; but he didn't care.

And Ma stood up and said, "Come and help me plant some rice!"

"Kiss me ass!" Pa said.

"But I have to go and see Balraj and Rama in dat haspital."

"Just shut dat mout I say!"

Ma was helpless and afraid. She wasn't a coward or anything; she was brave, but brave only as a woman is brave. Like the time last year when Balraj went to steal oranges in Sancho Estate, he carried Rama with him. The rain was falling and falling and falling, yet Balraj carried Rama with him. There was thunder and lightning and the sky was dark; Balraj carried the empty ricebag on his shoulder, and Rama walked behind him. The orange tree was tall. Many lianas were choking the tree to death. Balraj climbed up, picked the oranges and threw them to the ground for Rama. Rama collected the oranges and threw them inside the ricebag. But Rama started to bawl, bawl as if something was biting him. Balraj climbed down the tree, because he thought that a snake was biting Rama. Rama was bawling and rolling on the ground but nothing was wrong with him. Balraj grew afraid. He left Rama inside the estate alone. He ran home through the rain and told Ma that a spirit was holding Rama under the orange tree. Ma ran into the estate and found Rama rolling under the orange tree. He told her that there was an evil spirit upon him; the spirit was biting and choking him all the time. Rama was fighting her, but Ma was strong. And when she brought him home he was still bawling; bawling because the spirit had followed him into the house. Ma fought with him all night. In the morning he was better, because Ma had the strength to drive the spirit away.

"Come and help me plant de rice," Ma said.

"Why?" Pa asked, still sitting.

"Because I want to go in dat haspital and see Balraj and Rama. I is dey modder."

"Now you shut you modderass and plant dat rice!"

Pa stood up. He stood up as a tall juniper stump. His belly was full of the mangoes he ate, so he had the strength to watch Ma. Ma was hungry, so she couldn't quarrel too much. She just loosed another faggot and went on planting the rice.

Sunaree was planting good, but not good enough. Her rows were not in one straight line; she was trying her best to make a straight line, but she couldn't. When Pa shouted at Ma, Sunaree looked for Panday. He was still trying his best to rescue the reddish crabs.

"Panday come and help me plant de rice!"

"I not helpin you plant no rice!"

"Panday Pa goin to beat you," Sunaree warned.

Panday knew that Pa was a snake. He left the crabs alone, took a faggot and went toward Sunaree. Panday was not a good planter; he didn't know how to ram the rice roots under the water and then cover them with mud, but he was trying to plant faster than Sunaree. He wasn't holding the plants carefully; sometimes he squeezed so hard that they broke in the middle just about the water line. There was about eight inches of water in the riceland. The rice plants were about sixteen inches long; when the roots were buried in the mud, the plants were supposed to stand straight above the water. Panday finished his faggot quickly and took another one. But he was afraid; afraid because some of the rice plants he had planted were leaning in the water; others were buried so deep into the mud that the tops were hidden under the muddy water; some of the plants just floated above the water.

"Look wot you doin Panday!" Sunaree said.

"I not doin notten. Dis rice coud kiss me ass! I is a chile."

"If Pa hear you he go beat you Panday!"

"But I is a little chile!"

Pa stood on the riceland bank by the doodoose mango tree. He heard Panday. He jumped as a bull on the riceland bank. "Panday shut you kiss me ass mout boy! Shut it boy! Me Jesus Christ! If you make me come in dat wadder I go kick you till you liver bust!"

And Ma: "You leff dem chirens alone! Just leff dem alone! Befo you send dese chirens to school, you makin dem plant rice in Tola. But I tell you dat God watchin from dat sky. Dese chirens goin to come man and woman in Tola. Just leff dem alone!"

There was no more race between Sunaree and Panday now. Speed was getting Panday into trouble. He stooped down and moved as an old man in the water, but he still couldn't make a straight line.

Then Pa left. He walked slow because he didn't want to fall on the slippery bank. He went home.

The time passed slow, but it passed. The evening walked out of the forest and hunched over Tola. Ma had the last faggot. Birds moved hurriedly from one corner of the sky to the other. Thousands and thousands of birds: doves, semps, silverbeaks, wild pigeons and hawks just floated across the sky; they passed over the riceland, hurrying to their homes inside the forest. The clouds were tired in the sky; they floated about lifelessly.

"Sunaree and Panday go home," Ma said.

Sunaree and Panday were tired and hungry; their bellies were full of wind; they were getting sharp pains in their stomachs, but they waited for Ma. Ma was in a great hurry to finish the last faggot; she too was hungry and tired. When the last faggot was planted Ma came out of the water.

Pa was asleep on a ricebag near the rainwater barrel. He was snoring *hort snort hort snort* like an animal. His mouth was open. Flies went inside his mouth, but they came back out because his mouth was smelling bad. His hands were folded across his chest as if he was already dead; dead and rotting.

Ma took the enamel dipper. She fished out some water from the rainwater barrel and poured it over Sunaree and Panday. They rubbed their skins, trying to get the mud off their bodies.

Pa woke up. "All you makin too much kiss me ass noise!"

"Now is evenin," Ma said. "You not sleep enuff?"

"No!"

"You come home a long time now. You not plant no rice. You know full well dat dese chirens hungry. Befo you cook some food, you studyin to sleep."

"You shut you kiss me ass mout and cook!"

"I cant cook! I have to go and see Balraj and Rama in dat haspital."

"You shut you ass and cook!"

Pa went on talking; he talked *vat vat flap flap flap* as when a jandi pole shakes in the wind. There were razor grass and broken bottles in his voice. Pa talked; he didn't talk a little and stop, and talk a little and stop; he just went on talking and talking and talking. Ma was quiet; she just shook her head from side to side as a mad woman shakes her head.

"Come inside de kitchen," Ma said to Sunaree and Panday.

Ma walked into the kitchen first. Sunaree and Panday walked behind her; they looked back all the time, because they were afraid of Pa.

"Put some water in dat iron pot," Ma said to Panday.

Panday took the pot and went by the rainwater barrel.

Sunaree was helping Ma knead the flour. Ma sat on the earthen floor and peeled sweet potatoes with a small knife. Most of the potatoes were reddish and rotten like.

"I want some water for de flour Ma," Sunaree said.

"Ay Panday!" Ma called.

There was no answer. Ma called again. There was no answer. As she was about to call again, Panday ran inside the kitchen.

"Wot happen boy?" Ma asked.

"Pa runnin me wid de ledderbelt!" he said.

Ma lifted her head. Pa stood in the doorway as a dead tree. He had the leather belt in his left hand; he was gripping it firmly. "I go kill Panday ass!"

Sunaree had dry flour in her hands up to her elbow. She was sitting on the wooden peera. She was no longer kneading the dough to make the roti; her fingers stuck to the flour, and with her head tilting slowly backwards, she stared at Pa in fear and disgust.

"Now you leff Panday alone!" Ma shouted.

"Why?"

"Because he is my chile. I bleed blood to make him. You dont want me to go and see Balraj and Rama in dat haspital.

But I goin walkin to Tolaville. You cant stop me. Dem chirens longin to see dey modder. I goin walkin to Tolaville I tell you!"

There was a slow groaning as if a cow or a mule were groaning; groaning in sleep like. Ma sank to the ground as level as a shadow. She held on to her head and groaned sharply. She wasn't bleeding or anything. Pa just struck her in her right ear with his huge fist.

"Now Panday come here!" Pa screamed.

Panday leaned against the wall as if he was a wall too, leaning against another wall. With tears in his eyes he begged Pa saying, "Wen you get old I go give you food! Dont beat me Pa!"

"Panday!"

"Yeh Pa."

"Siddown!"

"Oright."

Panday bent his knees and leaned against the wall. His lips shook. Saliva leaked out of his mouth and ran down his neck. He watched Pa. Sunaree sat in front of him; her back was almost touching him, but Panday couldn't see her, because he just watched Pa.

Ma got up slowly. She held on to her right ear.

"Like me ears bell bust!" she screamed.

"You shouda dead!" Pa yelled.

"O God! Me ears ringin inside."

"You shouda dead," Pa declared again as he walked out of the kitchen.

After a while Ma loosed the floursack from her head. The floursack was spotted with dirt. She sat down, flung the floursack into a corner, and started to peel the sweet potatoes again. She had long black hair. Thick. The hair hung down from her head as strands of strong black rope. She wept as she peeled the potatoes; wept easy easy, because she was afraid to cry in the house.

Sunaree stood up. She went outside. The rice pot was sitting on an old potato crate by the rainwater barrel. She took it, dipped some water from the barrel and went back into the kitchen.

"Put de wadder to hot on de fireside," Ma said.

"Oright."

"Today you goin to see Balraj and Rama Ma?" Panday asked.

"No."

A little later and food was ready. It was a habit in the house: Pa always ate first. If he was not at home, Ma had to dish out his food first, then put it away. Ma took out a good portion of food and carried it inside the bedroom for Pa. He didn't say a word. He just ate the food.

VI

PA WAS ASLEEP.

Ma was picking Sunaree's head; each time she caught a louse she crushed it *tits* between her fingernails.

Nanna was running; he was blowing as a bull and running as a madman runs. He was moving fast. He bolted into the yard as a wild hog. His shoulder caught an orange branch; *crax!* the branch broke.

Ma pushed Sunaree aside. "Wot happen Pa?" she asked.

Nanna was still running; he was wearing a white merino and running like the wind. He passed by Ma like a lightning and ran by the ricebox, then he turned around as a snake turns and ran back by Ma.

"Rama dead! He dead and gone!"

"O God! O God! Me chile God!!!"

And Nanna: "He get over de skopian bite, but he dead wid umonia fever. He just dead. I runnin from Tolaville."

The sun was low as a house and red like a jamoon; it looked as if it was falling inside the Gulf of Tola. Pa was resting on the ricebags inside the house. He was awakened by the bawling. He listened. Rama was dead. His head began to beat like a drum. He got up and ran out of the bedroom as a rat.

Ma saw him. "You drink rum and run me chile in dat rain. But it have a God I tell you. I go tell de whole of Tola dat you kill me chile! Now he dead and lyin down in Tolaville."

Pa folded his arms. "Is true I drink rum. But me eh kill dat chile. Me eh de know de chile wouda dead. God kill

Rama. I didnt run dem in dat riceland to kill dem. I de just run dem because me eh de want dem to wet in dat rain. God know is de truth I talkin."

Nanna turned to them and said, "De chile done dead. Tink how to bury him. Tonight is de wake. Tink wot to do."

And Ma: "Me son dead widdout seein he modder face. Two days he live in dat haspital just waitin to see he modder. He wait till he dead. Which part in dat sky you is God? Me chile not even leff a trace in de world. He just born and dead. Dat is all. And he own fadder kill him too besides!"

"I tell you God kill him!" Pa shouted. "Yet you sayin I kill him. Well me eh doin one kiss me ass ting for dis wake and funeral!"

Sunaree stood by the drain. She was crying and blowing her nose.

Panday was leaning against the tapia wall and laughing.

"Wot de ass you laughin for?" Pa asked him.

"I laughin because Rama cant pee on me in de night no more."

Pa didn't run up to him or anything. He just looked at him like a bull. Then Pa went and stood in the yard.

The sun jumped inside the sea to sleep and the night crawled as a fat worm over the face of Tola. Nanna and Nanny were busy making flambeaux and putting them all over the place. Ma kept inside the kitchen as if she was sick or something. Pa didn't move from the yard.

The villagers came; they came from Tola Trace and they came from Rajput Road; they came from Karan Settlement and they came from Lima Road. Nanna gave some of them money to get rum and biscuits and coffee to keep up the wake. The house was crowded; the villagers knew Rama was dead, so they came to drink rum and talk.

A tall villager called Jadoo said to Pa, "Trobble is for everybody. De boy done dead. Wot you coud do now."

Then Benwa the greatest stick-fighter of Tola said to Pa, "Wot you goin to do Babwah. Trobble is for everybody."

Jadoo moved away and went inside the house and joined the villagers, because he and Benwa were not friends.

A short one-legged villager handed Pa a bottle of rum saying, "You eh have to worry too much. Keep corage. You just have to ride you wife and make anodder chile."

Pa didn't answer. The one-legged man chuckled and came into the house.

A little later the village priest came. He was thin as a whip. With his long white beard and sunken eyes, he looked as a jumbie. The villagers stood up and greeted the holy man. The priest spat out some blessing and sat down on a potato crate.

"Where Babwah?" the priest asked.

"I goin to get him Baba."

Jadoo went out into the yard and came back with Pa. Pa sat down next to the priest.

Some of the women were inside the kitchen. They were helping Nanny to keep Ma quiet. Ma was really getting on; bawling and getting on like a sick cow. But most of the women sat with the men, because they wanted to drink plenty rum and talk like men.

Pa sat next to the priest and talked. He was busy telling the villagers how Rama was a harden child — the hardenest child in Tola; how he played in the riceland everyday and got wet in the rain; how he was a spoilt child — Ma spoilt him; he got sick and died because he was too harden. The villagers drank rum and listened, and they felt sorry for him.

A Madrassi woman named Jasso lifted her dress above her knees and said to Pa, "You chile done dead. You eh have to worry. You coud sleep wid me a few nights till you worries past."

And the one-legged villager said, "Dat woman want a good man in she ass!"

And she: "Ay man, watch you one foot ass. Wen I want a man, I want a good man. Me eh want man like you."

"But I is a man. Dont mind I have one foot. De ting between me legs not cut out you know. It hangin dere just like befo."

"Man like you does take man befo dey dead!"

The Hindu priest wanted to make peace and help out the one-legged villager at the same time. He wiped his long beard and said, "All you lissen to me. Accordin to Hindu books, a woman is like a fire. A man is just like a old stick. Even if you trow one million firestick in a fire it never enuff. Even de wadder in de sea cant out de fire between a woman legs. De Hindu Bible make dis quite clear. A woman have room to take five men one time. I not sayin dese tings. De Hindu books say dese tings."

And Jasso: "A woman de made to take man. Wot you tink God make a hole between she legs for? God make a woman to take man."

"You go take donkey just now!" the one-legged villager shouted.

"I take donkey aready!" Jasso declared.

Inside the kitchen was full of people. They were sitting around Ma and talking. Ma was lying down on the earthen floor. She was trembling as if she was feeling cold. Her hair looked like a black mat nailed to the floor. A fat woman stood by her head and fanned her *voosh voosh* with a piece of cardboard. The woman was sweating and her body smelt as a rotten mango, but she fanned Ma all the time.

Then Pa came by the kitchen. He called the fat woman, "Ay Pulbassia."

"Oy!"

"I want to talk to you."

Pulbassia went out of the kitchen. Then she and Pa went in the yard. He told Pulbassia that Ma was worrying too much. He gave her a few bottles of rum for the women in the kitchen. Pa told her to give Ma a lot of rum to drink, because the rum was going to make her feel good.

"Oright," Pulbassia said, as she took the rum and went back inside the kitchen.

"Put some Bay Rum in de woman head," Pulbassia said.

"Oright," a woman said.

The woman went in the backyard and told Nanny that they needed some Bay Rum in the kitchen. Nanny left the coffee she was boiling and went inside the kitchen. She got some Bay Rum and handed it to the fat woman.

"How me dorta feelin?" Nanny asked.

"She go be oright in a little while," the fat woman said.

Nanny was too busy. She couldn't remain inside the kitchen to look after Ma.

As soon as Nanny left, the fat woman said to Sunaree, "Chile I goin to give you modder some rum. It go past she worries. If she drink a little bit, she go feel good."

"But Nanny say not to give she no rum."

"I go give she just a little bit. It good for she. It go make she strong."

The fat woman took out a bottle of rum. She opened it and poured a good drink into Ma's mouth. Then she took the Bay Rum and sapped her head.

"I go tell Nanny you give she rum," Sunaree said.

"Little girl haul you ass outa dis kitchen!"

"Oright," Sunaree said as she walked out of the kitchen.

Panday stood by the ricebox with his back resting against the cold tapia wall. He wasn't laughing now. His eyes were open like; just open and watching. Nanna walked up to him saying, "Wot happen Panday?"

"Notten man Nanna man. I just tinkin how Rama cant pee on me no more. He dead now. He have to live in dat riceland now. He have to hide good Nanna. If Pa catch Rama playin in dat wadder he goin to beat he ass wid dat ledderbelt."

He paused a long time to see if Nanna was going to say anything. But Nanna didn't talk. Panday went on, "We go put him in a ricebag. But if he want to come outa dat bag, wot we goin to do?"

"He done dead Panday. He goin to bury under dat ground in de mornin."

"Which part Nanna? Under de lime tree by de latrine?"

"No. He goin to bury in Karan Settlement in de bellin ground. Dat is de place dey does bury dead people."

"But me and Sunaree coud bury him under de lime tree. But sappose a snake bite him in de night Nanna?"

"He cant feel notten. He done dead."

"But sappose," Panday rubbed his eyes, "sappose Rama get up in de night wen me and Sunaree bury him? Sappose he tief lime and sell in Tolaville Nanna?"

"Rama goin to rotten under dat ground. Rotten just as a dog rottenin."

"Balraj goin to rotten like a dog too Nanna?"

"No."

Panday leaned against the wall sadly. Nanna went in the backyard to talk to Nanny.

"It never had a prettier woman dan Ama in Tola!" the one-legged villager shouted.

Madrassi Jasso disagreed strongly. She argued that Soomintra, the woman who married Sankar, was the prettiest woman in Tola.

"Shit talk! Shit talk!" the one-legged man shouted. "Soom-intra good lookin, but she not better dan Ama. Ama half white you know." He wiped his face with his shirt and continued, "Ama half white. But dat is not all. She have backside dat big and soft. Ama is de best woman I say."

"You shut you one foot ass!" Madrassi Jasso shouted. "I sure you never ride a woman in you life. De day a woman lie down for you, you go run like a mule. You modderass one foot bitch!"

"Well you lie down for me nuh. Do it and see if wouldnt trow some good wood on you."

And the priest: "Lissen to me. Ama is de dorta of de white-man. But dat is not all. Look at Ramai. Ramai is de biggest man in Tola. He is Ama husban. Tola coud never have a pret-tier woman dan Ama. Wot de hell all you know? I married Ramai and Ama. I married Soomintra and Sankar. I know."

"Like you ride Ama aready Baba?" a woman asked.

"Have some rispek for me!" the priest said.

"Oright Baba," the woman declared.

Nanna came with coffee in a big pot. The coffee was smoking. Nanny passed around empty can cups. Nanna dipped a large can cup inside the coffee pot and poured coffee into the small cups which the villagers held. The villagers blew their coffee *flu flunx*, then they sipped *choot choot choot*. Benwa didn't take any coffee. The priest took a full cup and placed it by his feet. Then Nanny went into the kitchen and brought some salt biscuits. She passed the biscuits around. Benwa didn't take any.

"Take biscuit and coffee nuh Benwah," Pa said.

"No Babwah," Benwa said.

A little later Sunaree came with a wooden tray and collected the empty cups.

The night held on to Tola real hard. There were no stars in

the sky. Huge clouds like wet blankets stretched from one end of Tola to the other. But inside the house was bright. The flambeaux drank a lot of pitch-oil, but they made the place look good.

"Is time to hear a story now," the priest said.

"We go hear one from One Foot," the Madrassi woman said.

The one-legged man smiled and said, "I go tell a story about Jadoo. But I want Jadoo to give me de right away."

Jadoo said, "Is oright One Foot."

So the one-legged man said, "Well all you know Jadoo. He right in front all you eye. Well let me tell all you how Jadoo get dem cuts. All you know aready how he get dem cuts, but I still goin to tell all you.

"Jadoo de born in Sancho Estate. But he didn't want to work on de estate. He leave de estate and went to Jangli Tola. Now he went to Jangli Tola to make money. But trobble take Jadoo soon. One night he walkin by de trace near de swamp. He walkin quiet and good. Den he hear a man callin for help. So Jadoo say to heself dat a drunk man want to fight anodder drunk man. Well it had good moonlight dat night. Wen Jadoo gone closer, he see four men beatin one man. Well Jadoo get vex one time. He tell dem to stop beatin de man. Wen de four men hear Jadoo talkin two of dem run like hell. Den de man dey de beatin get up and run too. But two of de men decide to fight Jadoo. Well Jadoo de young and brave. So Jadoo decide to fight. One of de men had a cutlass and one had a stick. De man wid de stick hit Jadoo one. As Jadoo lean in front de man wid de blade chop him on he head. Jadoo start to beg dem and tell dem he from Tola. But dem men de drunk like hell. De man start to beat him wid de stick. Every time de stick hit Jadoo, de man wid de cutlass chop same time. Nine time de man chop Jadoo in he hand. Den de man chop Jadoo big toe. Well Jadoo de know dat dey goin to kill him. He grab de stick and he hit de man wid de blade one stick. De man fall. Den Jadoo run in de mangrove. Dem two men look for Jadoo wid lights, but Jadoo get away. So Jadoo come back to Tola. I not lyin. Look Jadoo right dere."

The villagers were quiet. It was as if they were thinking about what the one-legged man told them. Soomintra was the first to speak. "Wot make you come back to Tola?" she asked Jadoo.

"I come to Tola because I want a son."

"Dem tings is lie!" a young man shouted.

And the one-legged man who told the story said, "Tola changin! Dese young modderass people runnin away from Indian ways. But dey go sorry. In dis same Carib Island and Indians goin to catch dey ass!"

"Shut you one foot ass!" the young villager shouted.

Jadoo got mad. "Shut you ass!" he shouted at the young villager. "Watch me good! I go hit you one kick and bust you kiss me ass chest!"

Jadoo got up to hit the young villager. But the village priest said, "All you stop dat. Dis is a wake all you know."

Nanny kept pushing logs inside the fireside. She had to keep the coffee boiling all the time. She looked tired and sleepy, but she had no time to rest. Sunaree took the pokanee and blew at the fire. The coffee beans were going *cruk cruk* inside the pot. Sunaree's face was red, because she was sitting too close to the fire. "Move from in front of de fire," Nanny said.

"Oright."

Sunaree moved a little and sat on a ricebag. She looked at Nanny and asked, "But wot goin to happen to Rama wen dey bury him in dat ground Nanny?"

Nanny lit a cigarette. "Well God goin to come down in dat cemetry and carry him in de sky to live."

"But sappose he fall from de sky Nanny?"

"No beti. God goin to take care of him."

"Wot about if de Devil turn him to a horse and ride him in de night."

"He is a little chile. He not have no sin. He goin straight by God."

Then Nanna came into the backyard and joined them. "You want coffee oldman?" Nanny asked.

"Me eh want none," Nanna said. "It about time Babwah go to Tolaville and bring up Rama. De nurse say de chile have to come home tonight."

Nanny told him not to bother Pa at all. She told him to go to Tolaville for Rama. Nanna told her that the nurse said that the father was the one to come for Rama.

"Well just go and tell de nurse," Nanny said easily, "tell de nurse dat de chile fadder worried. Dat is all."

"Oright."

Nanna went inside the house and said, "Who want to go wid me and bring de chile from Tolaville?"

"I go go wid you oldman," stick-fighter Benwa said.

Nanna and Benwa jumped on a horse cart and left for Tolaville.

The women in the kitchen were having a good time. They were excited; getting on like crazy ants; talking hard and running all over the place. Ma was still on the ground; she was drunk and talking about Rama.

The fat woman called Pa. "You wife not restin at all," she said.

"Give she some more rum. Rum go help she to feel good."

Pa went back to listen to the stories. The fat woman called, "Ay Jasso!"

"Oy!" Madrassi Jasso answered.

"Come dis side nuh gal. Wot de ass you doin by de mens all de time?"

Madrassi Jasso came inside the kitchen. She saw Ma on the ground, so she asked what was wrong with her.

"She mind worryin she too bad," the fat woman said. "But she husban give me some rum to give she. She go feel good just now."

The fat woman took a drink and passed the bottle to Madrassi Jasso. She swallowed a few drinks *gluk gluk gluk*, and passed the bottle to the other women in the kitchen. "Time to hear a story," Jasso said.

"Oright," the fat woman declared.

Pulbassia was the name of the fat woman. She told the other women to move and make room for Jasso to sit on the floor. The drunken women shifted a little, and Jasso sat down. "Gimme anodder drink befo I start," Pulbassia said.

When she got the drink she began to tell the story. "Well all you womens know dat Ama is a jamet. Man never enuff for she. All you see dat Pandit who siddown outside dere. He just playin priest in Tola, I tell all you. One night up in Sancho Estate, Ama de want a real good man. So she wake up she husban Ramai in de night. Wen Ramai ask she wot happen, she tell she poor husban dat she have a spirit on she. Well all you know how Ramai like Ama. Ramai take Ama dat late hour in de night and bring she down Rajput Road to meet dat same Hindu priest sittin down outside dere. Ramai wake up de Pandit and tell him dat he wife have a spirit on she. De Pandit lissen good, because all you know Ramai is a big man in Tola. But de Pandit de know dat Ama de just want a good man in she ass. So de Pandit tell Ramai to go outa de house and leave he and Ama alone. Ramai leff de house. As soon as Ramai leff, dat priest outside dere just pull Ama down on de bamboo settee. Man I tell all you, dat priest start to make ruction. He put

Ama down and trow able ledder on she. Well de Pandit give she good in she tail. After dat Ama leff and come outside. Den de priest come outside too. Ramai ask de priest if de spirit gone. De priest laugh and say de spirit gone. Den Ramai take he wife to go back home. But de priest call him and tell him to bring he wife every week for a check up." Then she asked Jasso, "You tink dat old priest coud ride a woman?"

And Jasso: "Dem Hindu Pandit and dem does eat butter. Dey does drink milk. Dont hot you head nuh. Pandit does look for dey little womens like anybody else yeh."

But dat Pandit so old man," a woman said.

Pulbassia said, "Old! Dat Pandit face only old."

It was almost midnight. Some of the women were going to sleep on the earthen floor in the kitchen. Pulbassia held a bottle of rum in her hand, and said, "All you womens drink de kiss me ass rum nuh!"

The women loved rum. They sat up and continued to drink again.

The men were telling stories on the other side too. There was plenty of joy in the house. Pa was laughing hard hard and enjoying himself. It was the priest's turn to tell a story. But the priest was complaining; talking easy easy and saying how he was not feeling well. "Dont play de ass Baba," Pa said, "tell we de story man."

"Oright," the holy man said.

With opened mouths the villagers waited to hear the story. The priest studied them a little, then he told the story about John Sharp the whiteman, and the grandfather of stick-fighter Benwa. Benwa's grandfather was called Karan. He came to Carib Island in 1845. Then Karan went as an indentured labourer on Indian Estate. John Sharp was the overseer. Karan was a very strong man. He finished serving his bound in 1850, but he remained on the estate and continued to work with the whiteman. In 1855 when the whiteman left Indian Estate and came to Tola, he brought Karan with him. Then Karan left Tola and went away. Many years later Karan came back to Tola with a horse cart. He lived at the whiteman's house.

Everyday Karan used to take the horse cart from Rajput Road and go to the Carib Mountains. For years he brought stones and dropped them in Tola cemetery. Then the whiteman and the grandfather of stick-fighter Benwa went to Spanish City, and brought another whiteman to Tola. The strange whiteman built a tomb. Soon after that Karan died, and John Sharp and the strange whiteman from Spanish City buried Karan in the tomb. Then that section of Tola was called "Karan Settlement." So the grandfather of stick-fighter Benwa will remain a mystery in Tola, because he was a great man.

The priest pursed his lips and watched the people.

Then Jadoo folded his arms and said, "Me eh tink dat Karan was so great."

The other villagers were afraid to talk back to Jadoo, because he was one of the fighters of Tola. But the one-legged villager winked saying, "Jadoo you wait till Benwa gone wid de oldman to Tolaville befo you talk so. You coud say wot you want. But Karan was a great man I tell you."

The priest knew that Jadoo was a hot-blooded man, so he said, "All you pass around some cigarettes nuh. Get some coffee and ting for de people."

Pa realised that Ma was drunk enough. He got up and went inside the kitchen. Ma was sleeping on a ricebag. He folded his arms and said to Pulbassia, "Everyting oright in here?"

She laughed and said that everything was all right.

"Well tell we someting about you dead son, nuh," Jasso said.

Pa folded his arms and talked to the village women; they folded their arms and listened; they listened with their eyes open and their mouths wide open. Pa told them how he loved children, especially Rama; telling them how he used to bathe Rama, wash his clothes, and put him to sleep at night. Rama loved him so much, and he loved Rama too. He used to work like a bull. He loved work so much that at times he never bothered to eat. He used to work day and night in the riceland: cutlass the lagoon and fork up the dirt from sunrise to sunset, all this he used to do because he loved his children. He bought the most expensive clothes for his children, but they threw the clothes away. Now Rama was dead. He was not to blame. Ma was bad. She was a rum drinker; she used to drink rum night and day; she used to hide the rum inside the ricebox; sometimes she hid the rum inside the riceland. Rama got sick because Ma sent him to hide rum inside the water. Ma was a careless woman; she had no love for her children; none whatsoever, and this was the reason why Rama got sick and died in the hospital. The night Rama got sick Pa carried him to Tolaville Hospital on his shoulders; rain was falling and there was thunder all over Tola, yet he carried Rama on his shoulder to the hospital. When he put Rama in the hospital, he walked back to Tola Trace for Balraj. He did this because he loved his children. That night Ma was drunk and sleeping; she didn't even help him change the children's clothes. So the village women listened and listened, and tears fell from their drunken eyes as they listened; they felt sorry for Pa, so they moaned for him as they listened and listened, and Pa talked and talked.

Pa kept his eyes on the ground. He wanted to be certain that Ma was drunk enough.

Nanny could have told the village women a different story, but she was too busy in the backyard boiling coffee. Pa had to be careful. Nanny had to be out of the kitchen in order for him to talk.

Jasso held Pa around his waist and said, "Look at de poor man." Pa smiled a little because he was feeling good like. "Eh, look how dis poor man worryin about he chile. I tell you. Look how he wife drunk!"

"You go take a little drink?" Pulbassia asked Pa.

"Yeh. I go take a little little one wid all you womens."

Pa took a little drink, looked at Jasso's hips a little and then he went outside.

"Past some rum around nuh man," a villager said to Pa.

Pa said sadly, "Is me son who dead. Me mind worryin me bad. All you help all you self nuh."

"Sorry bredders," the villagers said.

Pa sat close up to the priest. He told the holy man how Ma was drunk in the kitchen. The priest took out he eyes and said, "But you wife playin in she ass really. You mean she son dead and she drinkin rum?"

"Yeh Baba."

Their talk was cut short. Nanna and Benwa reached with Rama. The horse crossed over the drain and pulled the cart into the yard.

There was plenty of excitement in the house. The sober villagers ran out into the yard and the drunk ones stirred in their sleep. The women left Ma in the kitchen and went into the yard to see the child. They were shubbing each other and talking kind of drunk like. Nanny and Sunaree left the coffee in the backyard and ran by the cart also.

Rama was on the cart all right. Just dead and lying down stiff. He was wrapped up in white sheets; he looked like a sack of flour. When Nanny saw Rama, she started to bawl. "O God! Look how me grandchile dead!"

And Nanna: "Hush you mout. He done dead aready."

But Nanny couldn't shut her mouth; Rama was already dead but she couldn't shut her mouth, she kept on saying that Rama was a child and God had no right to kill him.

The village women were putting on a show. They held their breasts and rubbed their bellies and cried; they cried and cried; rum made them cry, they cried loud loud and blew their noses *tort tort tort*. Jasso jumped as a monkey and said, "Look at de poor little chile."

Pulbassia scratched her behind and groaned.

The one-legged villager rubbed up against Jasso saying, "I in de mood gal."

The village priest was getting on like a madman; he pulled his white beard this way and that way; he shook his thin body this side and that side; then he farted and said, "Bring de chile in de house."

A woman hawked and spat on the ground saying, "Dat kiss me ass priest guts like it rotten!"

Nanna forgot himself. He just stood by the cart and looked at Rama. He didn't even hear the priest when he said to take the child into the house.

"Dowlat!"

"Yeh," Nanna said.

"You eh hear me say to take de chile in de house," the Pandit said.

Nanna and Benwa brought Rama into the house. They put him on the ricebags near the ricebox. Then the Pandit recited a few mantras over him; he spat the verses fast fast. Nanna stood and listened to the mantras.

"Open de chile now," the priest declared.

With trembling hands Nanna removed the sheet from over Rama's face. Rama's face was bluish like a kohong's wings. It looked dried and long as a dog's face. His eyes were shut tight, but his mouth was slightly opened. Then Nanna called Pa. He came and stood near the ricebox.

"You have to touch de chile forehead," the priest said.

Pa bent down, touched Rama's forehead and moved away.

"Now he modder have to touch he forehead," the Pandit declared.

"But he modder drunk!"

"But she still have to touch he forehead," Nanny said.

Pulbassia and Jasso went into the kitchen to get Ma. She was still asleep. They shook her. She was too drunk. Grabbing her hands, they leaned her against the wall. She sat there without opening her eyes.

"Get up woman! You son in de kiss me ass house!" Jasso shouted.

"Dis woman son dead and she drunk," Pulbassia added.

"She lucky she have a husban like Babwah I tell you. He just wastin he time wid dis dry ass woman."

Ma didn't move.

Pulbassia took a cup of water and threw it *vash* in Ma's face. But it didn't help. Ma didn't even open her eyes.

"Well I never see dis modderass ting!" Jasso swore.

Nanny walked into the kitchen same time. She heard Jasso's remark. "Why all you womens dont shut all you tail! Me dorta is not a rum drinker like all you nuh. All you Madrassi bitches is de biggest rum drinkers in Tola. All you forcin rum down she troat all night, and now all you sayin she is a drunkard. But it have a God in dat sky. He seein all you."

The women didn't talk back to Nanny, because she was talking the truth. Nanny went to the rainwater barrel with the enamel dipper. She got some water and came back inside the kitchen.

"Which part I is?" Ma asked.

"You in de kitchen."

Pulbassia and Jasso giggled.

"If all you womens have to laugh, den go in de road and laugh. Dis house have a dead in it."

Nanny held Ma's hands. She lifted her a little. Pulbassia and Jasso watched. Ma stood up. She leaned against the earthen wall. She breathed deeply through her mouth; her breath smelt of rum. Nanny led her out of the kitchen. With great care Nanny helped her to the ricebox. Ma leaned against the ricebox, and Nanny sponged her face again.

Ma said, "O! O! Me head spinnin me."

"Touch Rama head. Dat is all you have to do."

When Ma heard Rama's name, she shook her head; opened her eyes; looked down.

"O God . . . "

"De woman drunk and de woman mad!" Pa shouted. "Move she away from here!"

And Ma: "You kill me chile. Rama was well well. You is de cause me chile dead today . . . "

"I tell all you de woman mad!"

And Pulbassia: "All you move de woman away from here. She drink rum and she only goin to make trobble."

Ma stooped down. She touched Rama's forehead; she touched it easy easy, then she grabbed it real hard. Nanny pulled her away; Nanny had a hard time pulling her away; Ma was strong; drunk and strong. Ma had fire in her eyes and the strength of a cow. But Nanny held her and pulled her as if she was tugging a bundle of green paragrass. Ma was strong strong. Nanny had to pull and pull. Ma gave up. Nanny guided her into the kitchen. Pulbassia and Jasso followed her into the kitchen. As soon as Nanny went into the backyard to see about the coffee again, Pulbassia opened a bottle of rum and pushed it inside of Ma's mouth. Ma made a lot of fuss, but Pulbassia put her knees on Ma's chest and poured the rum into her mouth. Then she pulled out the bottle. Ma shook her head from side to side; some rum fell on her thin neck, then she dropped flat on the ground.

At first Ma was a little restless; she turned from side to side like a sick dog; saliva leaked from her hard mouth and tears rolled out of her sad eyes. The women watched her as if she was a bad animal. Pulbassia spat on the ground and said, "If she just try to get up one more time, I go pour de whole bottle of rum in she mout."

Sunaree and Panday were sitting on a potato crate by the tapia wall; sitting and watching the villagers; sitting and watching Rama all by themselves. They were not crying; they were only sad like.

Nanna walked up to them. "All you want coffee?"

Nanna didn't even wait for an answer. He went in the backyard and got two cups of black coffee. He carried the coffee by the tapia wall. Sunaree took hers, but Panday said, "Me eh want none Nanna. It have a dead in dis house."

"Take it boy."

"Me eh want none."

"Why?"

"Because I not want none."

"But Rama is you bredder," Nanna reminded him.

"I still not want none."

Nanna knitted his brows. He thought for a long time. Then he told Panday how dead people were the best people, because they couldn't harm anyone. But living people were worst than cats and dogs.

"I know dat Nanna," Panday said.

"Well drink de coffee."

"Oright."

Sunaree and Panday emptied their cups. Nanna carried the cups for Nanny in the backyard. She took the cups and asked, "How Sunaree and Panday doin?"

"Dey doin oright." Then Nanna scratched his head and asked Nanny, "How me dorta drunk?"

Nanny put the cups down on the ground. She looked at Nanna sadly, then she told him about Ma. Ma was lying down on the ricebags in the kitchen. She was drunk, but she wasn't drinking the rum on her own will; she never really liked rum. She wanted to be sober; she wanted to be sober just to tell the villagers about Pa: tell them how he chased the children out in the rain and the wind; he ran them out of the house in the wind and the rain; tell them that he was drinking rum someplace in Tola when Rama got sick; just let the people know that when Balraj and Rama were stung by scorpions, Nanna went out into the night and searched for Pa; Nanna searched and searched, but he couldn't find Pa. But Ma couldn't tell the people anything. Pa like he knew that she was going to talk. He gave Pulbassia and Jasso bottles and bottles of rum; he gave them the rum telling them to keep Ma drunk; she was weak, he wanted her to sleep. And Pulbassia and Jasso were real rum suckers; they were glad to be in charge of rum, but they couldn't figure out why Pa wanted them to keep Ma drunk all the time. Nanny knew what was going on, but she couldn't do anything. All the other women in the wake were only interested in listening to stories and drinking rum. Nanny had to boil the coffee in the backyard because the villagers were quarrelling for coffee and rum all the time.

The villagers were quiet. It was as if they were still thinking about Rama. But the priest was eager to tell another story. He scratched his beard and said, "All you lissen to me. Now I go tell all you a story about Hoodlee."

"Tell we! Tell we!" the villagers shouted.

Just as the holy man was ready to begin, Nanna came again with a pot of boiling coffee. Nanny carried the small wooden tray and shared out the biscuits. Pulbassia passed around the rum. When Nanna offered coffee to Jasso she said, "Oldman behave you ass nuh! It have rum here. You tink I go leff rum to drink coffee?"

"But you coud talk better dan dat," Nanna said.

"She talkin so because she want a good man," the priest declared.

Jasso lifted her dress above her waist. Her legs were long black and smooth.

The priest licked his lips and said, "You like you really hot tonight."

"Yeh. I want you to cool me down Baba."

"I old now," the priest cooed. "Besides I is a man of God."

Jasso sat down on the earthen floor. She took the rum bottle from Pulbassia and swallowed a few ounces. "It eh have notten better dan rum," she said.

"All you Madras people does drink de most rum in de world," the one-legged man said.

"Kiss me ass One Foot."

The priest lifted his hand. All the people became quiet. "I goin to tell all you de story about Hoodlee."

"Tell we! Tell we!" the villagers shouted.

"Oright. It had a time Hoodlee was livin in Karan Settlement. Dat was a long time now. Lissen good. All you open all you ass and lissen. Hoodlee de just finish servin he five years bound in Bound Coolie Estate. So Hoodlee de mindin some cows and workin for de white people too. Well in dem days, John Sharp was a big man in Bound Coolie Estate. He and Hoodlee was friends. Not close friends, but dey used to talk.

"Well Hoodlee had a big sapodilla tree in he yard. One day he de sittin down under de sapodilla tree and grindin he cutlass on a stone. Next ting he see is a old creole woman walk in he yard. She head was white white. She was so old dat she was walkin kind of bend like. Hoodlee see she, but he just sid-down under dat tree and play he eh see she. De creole woman come and stand up right in front Hoodlee. So Hoodlee raise he head and ask de woman, 'Wot you want mam?'

"'Me want a black neck fowl to buy.'

"Hoodlee get up. He watch de woman from head to foot. 'Oright mam. Me give you one fowl.'

"So Hoodlee hold de fowl. De creole woman give him one shillin. Hoodlee tell de woman he eh want de shillin.

"'Tank you,' de woman say.

"So de woman gone. But wen night come, Hoodlee was in trobble. He was bustin he head tinkin which part he see dat woman befo. Hoodlee tink and tink till he fall asleep. But eh. Hoodlee de never see dat woman befo. Next mornin Hoodlee get up early like hell to grind he cutlass again. Wen he bend down to sharpen de cutlass, he see one shillin in de ground. Now Hoodlee feel good. He take up de money and put it in he house. Den he gone to work. De next mornin he find anodder shillin by the sapodilla tree. So he say to heself, dat maybe de creole woman de drop two shillin by mistake. De next mornin Hoodlee find anodder shillin. Hoodlee take de shillin and gone back inside he house. Hoodlee say he not workin again. One shillin a day was enuff to keep him livin, because dat time Hoodlee eh de have no wife.

"Wen John Sharp de whiteman not seein Hoodlee comin to work, de whiteman make up he mind to come and see why Hoodlee not workin. So wen de whiteman come Hoodlee tell de whiteman dat he sick. He eh tell de whiteman notten about dat money he was gettin. De whiteman de vex like hell, but he eh beat up Hoodlee. John Sharp just leff Hoodlee alone.

"But Hoodlee eh de have long again to collect dat jumbie money. One night he gone to sleep. He wake up in de night because he de only hearin tunder outside. Hoodlee watch good. He see he house door open. A whiteman walk inside de house. Now Hoodlee ass was cuttin nail. In dem days white people de bad like hell. White people used to beat people wid wip inside dey own house. So Hoodlee de tinkin dat John Sharp de come to beat him. So Hoodlee start to beg, 'Massa Sahib, me eh do notten. I go come to work Massa Sahib . . .'

"De whiteman walk up to Hoodlee. He had a handbag and a long black wip in he hand. He put he hand in de bag and take out a big chunk of gold. He offer de gold to Hoodlee. Hoodlee tremble like a leaf. 'Me eh want gold!' Hoodlee tell de whiteman.

"De whiteman offer Hoodlee dat gold three times. But Hoodlee eh take de gold. De whiteman take de gold and put it back in de handbag. Den de whiteman take de wip and he crack about fifty good lash in Hoodlee ass. Den de whiteman gone outside and crack dat wip so hard dat Hoodlee whole house de shake up. Next day Hoodlee gone to Bound Coolie Estate. He ask John Sharp if he de come and beat him last night. But it was not John Sharp who beat Hoodlee. Was a spirit dat beat Hoodlee. Dat was the last Hoodlee ever find money under dat sapodilla tree."

Nanna called Pa into the backyard. Nanny was still boiling coffee. "Ay!" Nanna said. Nanny almost fell inside the fire.

"Wot you want to talk about oldman?" Pa asked seriously.

Nanny offered Pa a cup of coffee. He refused it.

"I want to talk about de funeral," Nanna said.

"Talk. I lissenin."

And Nanna: "Now de priest go need some tings in de mornin. You have to go to Tolaville for plenty tings. Fust you have to get some good cattle butter. Den you have to get one yard of cotton. Den you have to get lohoban, gogool, camphor, and some white rice. And white merino to bury

Rama wid. Den you have to buy one coffin in Tolaville. Den after dat you have to go in de Warden Office and get de death certificate. Dat is all you have to do."

Pa was serious. "Oldman! You dorta feel I kill de boy. Well me eh doin notten. You want to bury him in coffin, den you buy coffin and bury him."

"But Rama is you chile man. He dead. Dis is de last you coud do for him. You go and get dese tings I tell you to get. Control youself man."

Pa was mad like a bull. "Kiss me ass oldman! You see about buryin him. I not takin me foot outa dis house."

"Well give me de money to bury him."

"Kiss me ass!" Pa said as he went back into the house to listen to the stories.

Then Nanny: "Dat man not goin to bury dat chile. How much money you have?"

Nanna dipped his hands into his pockets. He didn't have much money; it was his money that bought the rum, cigarettes, biscuits and coffee to keep up the wake. He counted the money. "I only have ten dollars."

"It not have no more money in we house home?"

Nanna said that there was no more money.

"Well," Nanny said, "buy de merino and de pants to bury Rama. Den buy de tings for de Pandit to do he work. You just have to leff dat coffin."

Nanna thought a little.

"I coud beg de carpenter in Rajput Road to come and make de coffin. He coud break de ricebox and make de coffin. I go tell him dat I go pay him wen I get pay."

"Well dat good. Try and see wot you coud do oldman," Nanny said.

Nanna harnessed the horse cart and hurried down Tola Trace.

The cocks were crowing *co kee yo ko! co kee yo ko! co kee yo ko!* all over the village. When the priest heard the cocks crowing, he jumped up. "Time to say some prayers for Rama." Pulling out his Ramayana, he went by the ricebox.

"Get a lota and some mango leaf."

"Oright Baba," Pulbassia said.

The priest took a mango leaf and sprinkled some water over Rama. Then he gave the mango leaf to Pulbassia. He took some flour and made a cross on the ground. The priest closed his eyes and recited some holy verses. Some of the villagers who were sober enough recited too. The hymn was long and strange. A strange silence came into the house. With closed eyes the priest recited on and on. Then he opened his eyes. "Gimme some flowers."

Pulbassia ran out in the yard and got some wild flowers. She handed them to the Pandit. "You want anyting else Baba?" she asked.

"Not right now."

The priest took the flowers and placed them on the sheet over Rama's chest. He closed his eyes and prayed for Rama's soul. His hands trembled as he prayed, and his body shook, and his voice was soft and powerful.

Pa stood next to the priest, but he didn't close his eyes. He looked at Rama all the time. While the priest was praying Pa bent down and kissed Rama on his forehead. Then he took his shirt and wiped Rama's face. Then he stood up and closed his eyes and prayed.

The village women stood around. Some of them were crying. Jasso wiped her eyes and said, "Look at de poor chile."

And Soomintra the wife of Sankar said, "It hard to bring a chile so big and den see it dead."

"All of we have to dead one day," Pulbassia declared.

Nanny was drooping in the backyard. The chants of the

priest woke her up. She rubbed her eyes. She listened. They were reading the sermon for the child by the ricebox. Nanny got up and ran from the backyard. She came and stood next to Pa. Nanny's face was old and full of wrinkles. Tears rolled out of her sunken eyes and fell on the ground. She listened to the chants.

Sunaree and Panday were asleep on two ricebags near the tapia wall; their mouths were open. A few cockroaches were walking over their bodies.

"Look how dem poor chirens sleepin," Soomintra the wife of Sankar said.

"Oh God! Dis world have trobble I tell you," Pulbassia cried out. Then she went by the tapia wall. She took two floursacks and covered Sunaree and Panday. Panday opened his eyes a little. "Sleep son," Pulbassia said. Panday closed his eyes and sank down on the bags again.

Then the priest tied some red strings around Rama's wrists to keep away the evil spirits. Putting a little flour on Rama's forehead, the priest called on the Aryan gods to look after the child. His voice was full of sadness, and the chants went up into the morning air as a special plea to God.

There was life in Tola. There was life in the wind as it left the corners of the sky and swept the face of the earth; there was life in the dawn that was coming with gold in its mouth; there was love in the night birds that made strange noises beyond the river; there was love in the people as their hearts reached up to the sky and their souls mixed with the void.

"Look at me grandchile!" Nanny screamed.

"Wot you go do?" Soomintra the wife of Sankar said. "Wot you go do woman? We born and we have to dead."

"But he is a chile."

"Everyting born on dis earth have to dead," the priest said. "De Hindu Bible say dat even de gods have to dead."

And Jasso: "Baba wen I dead I want you to do me work."

"Oright beti."

The priest read some more. The villagers wept as they listened. When the reading was over, the priest said, "Put de chile in de house."

Pa and Jadoo held the ricebags on which Rama was lying. They picked him up and carried him inside the bedroom. Jadoo came outside but Pa remained with Rama. Pa sat and stared at the child as if he was expecting Rama to get up and talk to him. But Rama just rested on the ricebags. "Come outside Babwah." Pa heard the priest calling him. Pa didn't move. He sat and stared into Rama's face.

The priest gripped his shoulders. "De boy done dead. Worryin not goin to help Babwah."

Pa and the priest walked away from Rama.

VII

SUNAREE AND PANDAY heard *hoosh hash hoosh hash see saw see* . . . They heard it inside their ears; they woke up.

The carpenter from Rajput Road was sawing board to make Rama's coffin. He had a yellow pencil stuck to his right ear. Jadoo and Pulbassia were holding the board across a wooden bench. Benwa and Pa stood with folded arms and looked on.

Sunaree and Panday got up. They went inside the kitchen. Soomintra the wife of Sankar was standing near to Ma. Ma was folded up in a corner; she was crying. Her mouth was open. There was a full bottle of rum sitting next to her. Many empty bottles were scattered on the ground. Nanna, Nanny and Jasso were there; leaning against the tapia wall.

"Nanny!" Sunaree called.

"Wot you want?"

"We just get up."

"All you hungry?"

"Yeh. Yeh Nanny, me and Panday hungry hungry."

Nanny gave them some biscuits and black coffee. Sunaree took hers, but Panday refused his again. He said that Rama was dead; Rama came inside the house and pissed in the coffee; he was not going to drink the coffee.

"Drink de coffee boy," Soomintra the wife of Sankar said.

"Me eh want none," Panday declared.

"Boy eat dat food!" Nanna shouted.

"Oright Nanna."

While they were eating Panday said to Sunaree, "You see wot I tell you. You see good. Rama smart like hell I tell you. He not by dat ricebox now. He get up in de night and hide away in dat riceland. He runnin whole night in dat wadder. But he better hide good from dem snakes. He runnin like a mule in dat wadder. But wen you see dem snakes get vex in dat wadder dey go eat he ass."

"Where Rama gone Nanny?" Sunaree asked.

"Rama not gone one place. He just lyin down in dat house. He goin to bury dis mornin."

"O God! O God!" Ma bawled out.

She tried to stand up. She fell *buff* on the ground. Nanny and Soomintra the wife of Sankar dragged her into a corner.

And Ma: "Where me Panday and Sunaree is? Dem too small to know wot happen in dis house."

Panday said, "Ma you drink rum and playin in you ass!"

Ma was getting on; bawling and swearing and getting on. Pa came inside the kitchen. "Keep dat bitch quiet!"

"But she chile dead," Soomintra the wife of Sankar said.

"Yeh. De chile dead, but she eh have to get on like a ass!"

Pa walked out of the kitchen.

The village priest was asleep on some ricebags. He was snoring like a bull. Flies settled on his face. Now and then he lifted his hands and drove them away.

"Bisnath Saddhu!" Benwa called.

The priest rubbed his eyes. "Wot you want?"

Before Benwa could say anything the one-legged villager said, "He is a modderass chamar and he playin Brahmin. Bisnath Saddhu is not a priest. He fadder used to mind pigs in Jangli Tola. He modderass chamar come to Tola playin holy."

And Pulbassia laughed and said, "Yeh One Foot. Give him in he ass!"

Bisnath Saddhu the village priest said, "Shut you one

foot tail! I not from Jangli Tola. Me fadder and me come from de Punjab."

"Punjab me ass Punjab!" Pulbassia shouted. "You son of a bitch Baba all you used to mind hog in Jangli Tola."

"Who say dat?"

"Me Pulbassia."

The priest sat up, wiped his eyes with the back of his hands, yawned and said, "I de born a Brahmin."

Bisnath Saddhu stood up. He was dressed in white, but his gown was dirty. He looked like a bird, but uglier than a white bird. Without even worrying about Pulbassia he walked up to the village carpenter.

"Sitaram Baba," the village carpenter said.

"Sitaram. How de box comin?"

"It comin good Baba."

The carpenter showed the holy man a crate. He sat down and sang bhajans. Then he called Pa. They talked a little about the funeral. Pa told him that everything was all right.

It was after nine when Nanna reached with the horse cart from Tolaville. The horse was trotting and the wheels threw dirt in all directions. The cart sang:

grang grang grang!
grang grang grang!
grang grang grang!

Nanna left the horse by the cashew tree and walked into the yard. Then he came into the house with a brown paper bag. "Sitaram Baba," he said, as he handed the paper bag to the priest.

The holy man peeped into the bag. "Oright," he said.

Nanna left the priest and went into the kitchen.

Ma was still drunk inside the kitchen. She walked to the fireside. Then she fell.

Nanna, Nanny and Soomintra the wife of Sankar held her and dragged her into a corner.

"Wot de ass all you doin?"

"Now stop talkin like dat!" Nanny shouted at Ma.

And Ma: "O God! My head hurtin me. Where Panday is? De rain fallin and dat rain wettin dem chirens. De modderass man is dey fadder. He runnin dem in dat rain. Look at dis house."

"Shut you ass nuh woman!" Madrassi Jasso shouted.

"Watch you mout Jasso!" Nanny said. "Is me dorta you talkin to. I is she modder and all you kinda Madrassi bitches and dogs cant talk to me dorta so."

Pulbassia ran inside the kitchen. "Wot happen?"

"De drunk bitch makin trobble!" Madrassi Jasso said.

And Ma: "De man runnin de chile in dat rain. De modderass man drinkin rum . . ."

Pa ran inside the kitchen. "Shut you kiss me ass mout! You drunkard bitch! You son in de house and befo you try to do someting, you drinkin rum. I go hit you one kick and break you kiss me ass back! You chamar modderass you!"

And Ma: "Now you want to kill me! O God de man want to kill me. He kill me son and now he want to kill me . . ."

"De man not doin you one kiss me ass ting!" Pulbassia said.

Benwa came into the kitchen. He said to Pa, "Babwah leff de woman alone!"

"I go beat she ass!" Pa shouted.

And stick-fighter Benwa got mad. His face became red. "Now Babwah if you beat dat woman I go put so much lix in you ass! If you want to fight, den fight me!"

Jadoo came inside the kitchen too. He and Pa were very

good friends. Jadoo just folded his arms and looked at Benwa. Benwa went on talking. And when Benwa finished, Jadoo said, "Benwa dis is de man house. If you want to fight him, you cant hit him in front of me."

And Benwa: "Me eh want to hit him at a wake! But Jadoo watch me good. Me eh want one hundred mens to stand up behine me befo I go in battle you know! I . . . "

"All you behave all you self," Sankar the husband of Soom-intra said.

The village priest came running inside the kitchen. "All you come outside and leff de womens in de kitchen."

They listened to the priest. Pa, Jadoo and Benwa came back by the village carpenter.

"Time to get de prayers goin," the priest said.

Pa, Nanna, Sunaree, Panday, Jadoo and Benwa and some of the women went inside the bedroom. Rama was lying on a white flourbag sheet. A deeya was burning by his feet, another was lighting by his head. The priest stood by Rama's head and recited some mantras from the Puranas and the Mahabharat. He recited as if he was quarrelling with God and quarrelling with the child; his voice sounded as if he was hungry or dying or something; his voice was heavy and it grated *crat crat crat* as if he had a cold; his breath was stinking so much that some of the villagers turned their faces away; a long line of spit came out of his mouth as a fat whitish cord; and the flies went *buzz buzz* trying hard to get inside his dirty mouth. When he heard his voice long enough, he stopped the recitation. He took the lota and sprinkled some water on Rama. "All you bathe him now."

Nanna went outside. He took a bucket and went by the rainwater barrel. Then he came inside the bedroom with the water. The priest said a few holy words over the water as if the water was dirty as his mouth. Now that the water was blessed Nanna removed the flourbag sheet that covered Rama's naked body. Rama was stiff as a piece of stick and bluish all over. There was a long cut running from his neck to the end of his belly; the cut was sewed up tightly. Just as Nanna was about to bathe Rama, the one-legged villager said, "Wait! He modder have to bathe him fust."

"But he modder drunk!" Pa shouted.

"She still have to bathe de chile," Sankar the husband of Soomintra said.

Sankar was a mystic from Gam Gam Tola. The village priest didn't like the way Sankar was siding with the one-legged villager.

"If he modder drunk, den she cant bathe him," the priest said.

"You is a chamar Baba! You not know you ass from you elbow!" the one-legged man shouted.

"I is a Brahmin!" the priest bawled out.

Pa took a piece of white cloth. He fingered it a little, then he dipped it *splunk!* inside the water. The cloth went *took took took* as the water wetted it. Pa wiped Rama's face and hands; he wiped slow. When he was satisfied, he passed the cloth to Sunaree. She was afraid to wipe Rama, so she merely touched his feet and passed the cloth to Panday. He was afraid. He just held the cloth and stared at Rama.

"Wipe him fast!" Pa shouted.

Panday just touched Rama's face with the cloth and handed it to Nanna.

Nanna kneeled down on the earthen floor. He took his time and wiped Rama. Then he turned him over and wiped his back as well.

"Good now. Put on he clothes."

Nanna had some trouble putting on the white merino for Rama; his hands were stiff like copper wire; Nanna had to bend them; bend them as if he was bending a piece of crappo board; bending the hands as if he was going to break them *crax!* But Nanna had no trouble to get the pants on him. Then Nanny handed him a small black comb. He took it and combed Rama's hair in a side part. Then Nanna put on a pair of white socks for him, and sprinkled a phial of essence on his face.

The priest called out to the carpenter, "De box ready?"

"Yeh."

"Make sure de foots face de trace. Dis chile have to leff dis house for good."

"Oright."

Then they came out of the bedroom, but Sunaree and Nanny remained inside the house with Rama. Then Sunaree said, "But Nanny."

"Wot you want?"

"Wen dey bury Rama in dat bellin ground, de Devil goin to ride him in de night."

"No. Rama goin right by God. Wen chirens dead, dey does go by God."

"So wot de Devil goin to do?"

"Dat Devil cant do notten. God goin to come down from dat sky. As soon as it get dark, God goin to come in dat cemetry and carry Rama to live in dat sky."

"And dat is because he done dead."

"Yeh," Nanny said.

"Den I want to dead too Nanny."

"Hush you mout, chile!"

The priest and the villagers came back inside the bedroom. The holy man sang some bhajans. Then Pa and Jadoo picked up Rama and carried him outside.

"Put de chile in de box one time," the priest said.

They put Rama inside the box. Nanny threw the black

comb inside the box with him. Then the priest winked and said, "Now is arti time."

Nanna brought a lota of water and handed it to the holy man. There were a few mango leaves floating in the water. Then Nanna went outside and got a taria. He held it in his hands. Nanny placed a block of camphor in the brassware and lighted it. The priest recited the sermon in Hindi as he sprinkled water on Rama. Nanna passed the taria to Pa; he passed it over Rama five times, then he handed it to Sunaree. Then Panday did the arti and gave the taria to Nanny.

The two villagers who were sent to dig the grave walked in the house. They had mud all over their clothes.

"Oright. Time for de burial," the priest said.

The priest and the villagers were becoming impatient; they were kicking their feet in the air like goats and scratching their bellies and grumbling.

"Take de chile in de yard."

"Oright Baba," Pa said.

The villagers carried Rama in the yard. Jadoo went by the cashew tree and got the horse cart. He brought the cart in front of the house.

"Put de chile on de cart now."

But they couldn't put Rama on the cart. Stick-fighter Benwa took his shirt and flung it in the yard. "He modder have to do de arti."

"But she kiss me ass modder drunk!" Pa shouted at Benwa. "Dowlat!"

"Yeh Benwa!" Nanna answered from inside the kitchen.

"Bring she out to do de arti."

Nanna and Nanny dragged Ma out of the kitchen. Soomintra the wife of Sankar went and helped them. Ma didn't even make an effort to get up, so they just dragged her through the mud in the yard and brought her to the box.

"Stand up!" Nanna said.

Nanny and Soomintra the wife of Sankar held her up. "O God me chile! Look how he dead. He fadder runnin him in dat rain. God you know . . . "

"Shut you modderass!" Pa shouted.

And Benwa: "Babwah if you touch dat woman today I go beat you! Let de woman cry over she chile."

The heavy clouds were moving in the sky and the thunder was beginning to shake Tola. The eyes of God were moving up and down in the sky and the lightning winked *zip zip* at the earth.

"Let she do de arti fast," the priest said coldly. "De rain goin to come."

Ma did the arti. Then she dropped the taria and held on to the box; she was holding on and getting on.

"Take she inside now!" Benwa said.

Nanna and Nanny dragged her back into the kitchen. Pa and Jadoo lifted the coffin and placed it on the cart. Nanny remained with Ma in the kitchen, but Nanna came back and sat on the cart. The priest sprinkled some water on the coffin again and said, "Drive now."

"Oright," Nanna said.

The villagers and Pa and Sunaree and Panday and the priest walked behind the cart; sometimes the cart went *plaps plaps* as the wheels went inside the deep holes. Each time the box tried to fall off the cart, the villagers pushed it back on the cart with their dirty hands. The trace was full of bamboo and basmatia grass, but the horse trampled over them *chich chich chich*, and the villagers walked *sich sich* behind the cart; they walked northward to Tola cemetery. When the cart reached the main road, Nanna drove the cart westward down to Karan Settlement.

"Stop here!"

The priest sprinkled some water on Rama, then he sprin-kled some on the road. "Drive now!"

Nanna drove the horse cart until he reached the small trace that led into the cemetery. He turned the horse to the north and carried the body in the cemetery.

"It didnt take long to come dem two miles," Pulbassia said.

"Dat is true," Madrassi Jasso declared.

Tola cemetery looked dismal even in daylight. Almost the whole cemetery was buried under tall bamboo grass. Huge immortelle trees and tall googloo trees grew on the northern side. There was a big tomb in the centre of the cemetery; KARAN was written on it.

The coffin was placed on the bamboo grass near the grave. The priest chanted softly. The villagers were sad and they were crying and getting on; Pulbassia was blowing her nose and saying, "A little chile like dis dead," and Madrassi Jasso said, "Look at de poor chile," and Nanna said, "He done dead aready," and the priest as if not listening to the villagers went on with the death sermon.

Benwa took a piece of camphor and went down inside the grave. He lighted it and came outside. Then he took another piece and lighted it on the northern side of the hole.

The priest called on the Aryan gods and commanded them to look down at Rama; so Rama was dead, but the gods were looking down at him; looking down and smiling.

"Nail up de box now!"

Nanna, Sunaree and Panday started to cry hard hard, but it meant nothing to anyone. The village women dried their eyes and looked on. The carpenter drove the nails *tap tap tap tap*, and Rama was shut in. They tied up the box with ropes and lowered it inside the grave. Then the people threw dirt *bup bup* inside the grave. Then Benwa took a shovel and Pa took a fork; they covered the grave up properly.

"Wen all you leff de bellin ground dont look behine all you backs," the priest said.

VIII

BALRAJ WAS OUT of Tolaville Hospital. His face was pale but he was feeling well. He dragged his hands in the water *wash wash*. Sunaree held the ricebag and Panday carried the cutlass. The cutlass was sharper than a razor grass so Panday had to be careful.

"Me eh know where dem crappo fish gone," Balraj said. "Just one week I stay in dat haspital and all dem crappo fish gone. Dey dead and gone just like dat."

"Dem crappo fish dead because Rama eat dem," Panday said.

"You hush you mout Panday. Rama done dead. Rat eat him in Tolaville haspital."

"Rama belly open like I tell you. He have a long cut in he belly. Rama hidin in dat wadder because he fraid Pa beat him."

"I tell you he dead and he still in dat hospital dead house. Rat eatin him."

"But last night I hear dem dogs barkin in de village. Dey barkin and goin *wow wow wow* whole night. Dem dogs runnin him all over de place."

Balraj stood up. He wiped his face with his dirty hands. A chunk of mud stuck to his right cheek. He looked up and saw the black clouds moving in the sky. The clouds were mad like; they ran into each other like mad bulls. Thunder rolled, but it rolled far far away; it rolled beyond the forest where the jumbies lived; it rolled over the mountains far away. The wind was blowing hard and cold. Leaves fell from the barahar tree and the wind dragged them inside the water. The leaves sailed like brown paper boats as they sailed in the riceland. Panday was crying in the water; he was crying easy easy. Balraj looked back.

"Wot happen Panday?"

But Panday didn't answer. He just stood in the water and cried.

"Wot you want Panday?" Sunaree asked.

Panday didn't answer; he just went on crying.

"Let we go under de barahar tree," Balraj said.

The barahar tree was on the south-eastern side of the rice-land. Balraj walked in front. Sunaree and Panday were just behind him. They were barefooted; they felt the grass pulling their toes. They walked southward through the riceland until they reached the long mango tree. Then they came out of the water and walked northward on the high land to the barahar tree.

The barahar tree was tall. Taller than a grass house but not taller than a mango or a carat tree. There were plenty leaves on the barahar tree; some of the leaves were thick and green, but some of the leaves were dry. Some of the branches were low, but not low enough to touch the ground. There were a lot of dry leaves scattered around the tree.

"Push away dem dry leaves wid de bag," Balraj told Sunaree.

"Why?"

"Maybe it have skopians in dem leaves."

Sunaree took the wet bag and swept the leaves away.

Then Balraj remembered something. He grabbed Sunaree. "You bitch! You kill dem crappo fish in dat bag."

"You pullin me hair Balraj!"

Balraj pushed her away. He peeped into the ricebag. He

couldn't see anything. He held the bag and shook it. Perhaps some tadpoles fell but he couldn't see them; the tadpoles were black and the sky was black; the tadpoles were black and the earth was black. "You kill dem crappo fish. You know I want to put dem crappo fish in dat hole I dig by dat coconut tree. Now dese crappo fish dead and gone."

Sunaree sat down under the barahar tree; her back rested against the heavy trunk. Panday sat on the ground and started to cry again; he was crying as if a jumbie was holding him. Balraj sat on the ground and said, "Cryin not goin to help. Rama done dead. Rat eatin him in dat dead house. So you stop cryin now."

"But Rama have a cut in he belly I tell you. He hidin in dat wadder from Pa. He goin to drownd in dat wadder Balraj."

"Rama not have no cut in he belly. He just dead. Dat is all."

"But me and Sunaree see de cut. It have a long long cut in he belly."

"All you not see notten. Dat haspital does smell like pee. Like cow pee I say. Dat night wen Nanna carry me and Rama in dat haspital was de fust time I see dat haspital. Wen we reach de hospital de creole wardman say, 'Me God! Look at de state of dese coolie chirens!' I tell all you. Huh. Dat nurse had on a blue dress. De creole nurse tell de wardman to put Rama on a long cot. De creole wardman put Rama on top of dat cot. But Rama de really playin in he ass. He just lie down on de cot and shut he eye. He de playin dead. So de nurse scratch she head and say, 'But dis chile sick bad.' Nanna de fraid like hell I tell all you. All you not see notten. De nurse and de wardman de busy like hell. Me and Nanna was watchin good. De nurse open a box like and take out one long injection. Den de wardman turn Rama over and de nurse push de long needle in he ass. Rama de playin man I tell all you. Dat needle went in he ass, and he didn't even bawl. Den de wardman get a kinda ting wid wheels. He roll it by de nurse. De ting had bicycle wheels, but dem wheels de flat like widdout air. Wen de ting was rollin it de goin *chooi chooi chooi* as a jumbie was bawlin. So dey put Rama in dat ting and roll him inside dat haspital."

Balraj took a long pause, swallowed some spit and continued. "Den was my turn. I tell de nurse dat skopian bite me just as how skopian bite Rama. So she make me lie down on de cot like. I de watchin dat nurse; watchin she real good. I was fraid like hell. Look nuh, I see dat nurse open dat box like and take out dat needle again. I start to get on wen I see dat needle. But dat wardman hold on to me. Den dat nurse push dat needle in me ass. I bawl out. Den de wardman put me on dat ting wid de wheels and roll me *chooi chooi chooi* to a bed in de haspital. I de feelin sick like hell. All you eh see notten, I say."

"Den why Rama runnin in dat wadder whole night?" Panday asked.

And Balraj: "You too stupid Panday! Rama dead. I know de night he dead. He was in dat bed next to me. Rama never even talk to me in dat haspital. I say to me self dat if he is me little bredder and he not talkin to me, den I not talkin to him too. Dat night was oright. De next day was oright. But in de night, early in de mornin he dead. Just befo he dead he siddown on dat bed. I say to me self dat he goin to talk to me. But he eh talk a word. He siddown on de bed, den he turn up he eyes, den he trow up and dead. Rama de coward too bad. He de fraid like ass I tell all you. Rama dead and dat nurse eh de know one ass. Dat nurse de tired. She de sittin by de table in de ward and sleepin. A old creole man in de ward call out and tell de nurse dat Rama dead. Wen de nurse hear dat Rama dead, she jump up as if she had a spirit in she ass."

"You eh de fraid little bit?" Sunaree asked.

And he: "Me name is Balraj! Me eh fraid notten. Den de wardman and de nurse wrap Rama up in a white sheet. Den de wardman bring de ting wid de wheel and carry Rama in de dead house."

Sunaree doubted him. Balraj was lying because Rama died; Nanna took a horse cart and brought Rama to Tola Trace; then there was the wake . . .

"All you cant fool me," Balraj said. "By dat haspital have big big rats. I see dem rats wid me own eyes. I tell all you dat Rama still in dat dead house in Tolaville. Rat eatin him. Nanna never bring Rama home. I never see Nanna bring dat boy on no horse cart. So Rama still in dat dead house. Rat still eatin him."

Sunaree and Panday protested loudly. They informed him how Nanna brought Rama from Tolaville in the night; he brought him on a horse cart. All the villagers saw him by the ricebox, they declared.

"All you stupid!" Balraj shouted. "All you cant fool me. I tell all you dat Rama still in dat dead house in Tolaville."

There was a long pause. The thunder rolled far away; far far beyond the mountains. Panday stood up.

Then Panday told his story. Balraj and Sunaree listened. He said Rama was living in the water. He drowned in the rice-land because he had a long cut in his belly. Rama was buried in the water. The water snakes were searching for him, trying hard to find him. The snakes were biting the mud with their long teeth and looking for Rama, because they wanted to eat him. The snakes were not moving by guess; they had friends, the scorpions. The scorpions stung Rama; Rama went to Tolaville Hospital and died, then Nanna went and brought him home. Rama was buried in the cemetery, but in the night he came out of the hole because he was hungry. Then he went inside the riceland because he was afraid of Pa. The scorpions couldn't come in the water to look for him; they couldn't swim. So Rama was living in the riceland; the snakes couldn't find him because they didn't know he was hiding in the water. Rama felt lonely in the cemetery and he was hungry too, so he came out. It was dark when he came out of the grave. But he couldn't come home just like that. He had to hide; hide from Pa and the villagers. At first he hid in the sugarcane fields, but the birds made strange noises. He was afraid of the birds; he thought they were going to eat him, because they were big big birds with long black wings. The birds were really jumbies; the souls of people who were dead. And Rama was lying down by the ricebox and listening to the stories the villagers told.

So when he came out of the grave he knew that the birds were jumbies who were going to eat him inside the sugarcane fields, so he came out of the cane fields. He tried walking home through the village, but he was afraid. The man in Jangli Tola took a cutlass and chopped Jadoo. Then Rama started to run, but the pariah dogs saw him and started chasing him. The pariah dogs were not really dogs. They were evil spirits that lived under the silkcotton trees in Sancho Estate; they were running him down to eat him. So Jadoo ran and ran from the dogs. Rama thought about coming home. But he couldn't come home. Ma was drinking rum and getting on and Pa was telling the villagers how he was going to beat him with the leather belt. Rama ran in the yard, but the dogs and the jumbies were behind him. He tried hiding by the lime tree but it wasn't safe enough. The evil spirits chased him. He ran inside the riceland. The long water snakes were dreaming; they didn't know when he came inside the water. The evil spirits were afraid to come inside the water; they were afraid of the snakes, but they stood on the riceland bank and quarreled hard hard. The spirits made so much noise that the scorpions woke up. The scorpions listened. They heard the spirits cursing and getting on. At first the scorpions were afraid of the spirits; they thought the spirits came to kill them. So the scorpions took their young ones and started running away; running and going deeper inside the forest. But the scorpions' young ones began to cry, and some of them were coughing. The evil spirits listened. So one of the evil spirits called out to the scorpions and asked them why they were running away. The scorpions said that they were afraid of the spirits. Then the jumbies told the scorpions that they were not going to eat them. The scorpions became brave. They came out of the bushes and talked to the spirits. The spirits told them how Rama was hiding in the water. The scorpions became mad with rage; they remembered how they stung Rama inside the ricebox. So the spirits went away into the forest. The scorpions stood on the riceland bank. They couldn't go inside the water, because the snakes were their enemies. The scorpions stood on the riceland bank and called and called and called, because the snakes were asleep. Then the snakes heard the scorpions. They answered. The female snakes told their husbands to be careful; the snakes told their husbands how a man chopped Jadoo in Jangli Tola in the night. But the male snakes only laughed at their wives, because they were not afraid of spirits and scorpions. The rain was drizzling; the male snakes didn't want to get wet; they wanted to cut some banana leaves, but they were afraid of their wives. Then the priest of the snakes told them that perhaps the scorpions were planning to kill them with a cutlass. The snakes believed the priest, so they told the scorpions to go away. But the scorpions told them that Rama was hiding inside the water. But the priest didn't believe that. He told one of the old snakes to go and hear what the scorpions had to say. The old snake grumbled as he went to the riceland bank. The scorpions were crying and telling the old snake how Rama was hiding in the water. The old snake ran back to the deep holes. He was blowing when he reached the holes. At first the snakes thought that the scorpions had beaten the old snake on the riceland bank; they were preparing to run out of the water and kill the scorpions. But the old snake told them that Rama was hiding in the water. The snakes knew that Rama was a harden child; he used to play in the water all the time. So the snakes began to search for Rama, but they didn't know that he had a long cut in his belly; they didn't know that he was buried in the mud . . .

Balraj and Sunaree listened. Balraj scratched his ears as he looked at the sky; the clouds were fighting with each other. Then he said, "Let we go and catch some more crappo fish. Wen dat rain come down, we cant catch none."

It was a good idea. They walked southward on the high land until they reached the long mango tree at the southern end of the riceland. There were many mangoes on the ground, but blue flies were sitting on them and singing *hm hm hm hm*. Sunaree and Panday picked up a few mangoes and washed them in a drain. They peeled the mangoes with their teeth as they followed Balraj into the riceland. They entered the riceland and started walking northward to meet the other colas. There were thick bamboo and basmatia grass in the southern section of the riceland. The last three colas were not cutlassed and forked up. This year Pa didn't plant any rice in the last three colas. Last year rice was planted in the southern section, but it was of no use. Last year Pa didn't want to plant any rice in the last three colas. But Ma quarrelled with him; quarrelled with him day and night; just quarrelled and quarrelled with him, because she wanted enough rice in the house; enough to sell and enough to give to beggars and enough for the children to eat as well. Pa didn't like the idea, so he remained home for many days without doing anything. But Ma was determined. She tied up her head with an old floursack, took the brushing cutlass and the crookstick and started to cut the grass. The bamboo grass were tall tall, taller than Ma in some places. The blade went through the grass:

swipe swipe swiping!
swipe swipe swiping!
swipe swipe swiping!

Ma only took a few days to cutlass the three colas last year. Balraj, Sunaree, Rama and Panday helped her clean out the colas. They threw the cut grass far away on the high land. Pa came one day and looked. The colas were clean. He tied the leather belt around his waist and forked up the land, then he levelled it with the white bull. Then Ma and the children planted the rice. But it was no use. The bamboo and basmatia grass grew faster than the rice. So when rice-cutting time came, there was no rice in the last three colas.

They walked until they came into the other colas. There were plenty tadpoles. The tadpoles were running and running; they were trying to hide from Balraj. Balraj was dragging his hands inside the water. There were hundreds of tadpoles in little groups; they were jumping and dancing in the water. Then Balraj heard *eh eh eh*.

Panday was crying; he was crying hard hard as if Balraj was killing him or something. But nobody was doing Panday anything. Balraj and Sunaree were scared. Pa was at home. If he heard Panday getting on like this, he was going to come in the water and beat them with the leather belt.

The rain was falling far away; falling on the high hills in Gran Couva. They saw the rain; it was like white smoke over the mountains.

Balraj found a way to keep Panday quiet. "Let we go by de coconut tree and see dem crappo fish in dat hole."

Balraj dug the hole the week before he went to the hospital. It was about time to see the hole. The hole wasn't deep deep. Balraj always had to hide and dig the hole. He took the old fork and hid it in the banana patch. Then he waited until Pa went into the village to drink rum. As Pa left, Balraj would run away from home. Sunaree, Rama and Panday didn't know he was digging a hole to put the tadpoles. But Rama found out about the hole; he couldn't keep his mouth shut, so he went and told Ma about it. Then one day Ma walked easy easy through the banana patch, then she passed behind the outhouse and went by the coconut tree. She looked. Balraj was digging the hole like a crazy man. Ma called. Balraj jumped up as if he was bitten by a snake. When he saw Ma he laughed and said that he was just digging a hole to put some tadpoles. Ma knew that Balraj loved the crappo fish, so she told him to go right on digging. It took him about three days to dig the hole. Rain fell almost every day, but the ground under the coconut tree was very hard. The coconut roots were red red; red like a centipede belly. Balraj had plenty trouble digging the hole. The coconut roots held on to the earth as eyes hold on to a cow's head. Balraj sweated and farted but he wanted the hole on the high land. He knew the heavy rains were going to come down soon; he wanted the hole away from the riceland. When the hole was ready Sunaree, Rama and Panday helped Balraj to fill up the hole with riceland water. But the hole was greedy as a quenck and thirsty as a cow; the more they poured riceland water into it, the hole went *frot frot* and drank up the water. But after a day or two the hole wasn't thirsty any more. The rain came down heavy heavy in the night and the hole had enough to drink. Then they caught the tadpoles and threw them in the water.

A dry coconut branch was covering the hole. Balraj pulled the branch away and peeped into the hole. Thousands of tadpoles were dancing in the water. Balraj laughed. "Dem crappo fish glad nuh ass to see me. I is like dey fadder, because I mindin dem in dis hole."

"Dey glad to see me too," Sunaree said.

Balraj and Sunaree laughed and felt good. But Panday was sad sad.

"Wot happen Panday?" Balraj asked.

"Maybe Rama in dat hole. He still hidin in de mud. I goin in dat hole and tell Rama to come out."

"But you goin to kill dem crappo fish if you do dat."

"I still goin in de hole."

"You cant do dat."

Panday started to cry and get on.

"Oright," Balraj said, "I goin to ask dem crappo fish in dat wadder if Rama in dat wadder."

"Oright."

And Balraj sang.

crappo fish crappo fish in dat wadder
crappo fish crappo fish in dat wadder
crappo fish crappo fish in dat wadder
tell me tell me if Rama in dat wadder

Balraj held his right ear and leaned over the hole. The tadpoles danced and danced. He turned to Panday and said, "Dem crappo fish say dat Rama not in de hole. Dey say Rama in de riceland."

They remained a while by the hole. Balraj said that he wanted to see the tadpoles, because when the rain came again all the tadpoles were going to die in the riceland; they were going to live only if they were in the hole by the coconut tree. So they left the hole and went into the riceland water. Something went *splash!*

"Dat is a snake make dat noise," Balraj said.

They moved on again in the water; Balraj walked in front. There were a few tadpoles in the water but they were too small to put in the ricebag. Sunaree and Panday dragged their feet *pluck pluck pluck* in the water.

Sunaree and Panday obeyed Balraj. He knew the riceland much better than they did. They moved slowly. Sometimes they looked at the sky; the clouds were jumping up and down, fighting and threatening the earth.

They were near the deep holes. All the tadpoles were near the deep holes. They couldn't follow the tadpoles any more. They were afraid to go into the holes; afraid of the long water snakes.

Suddenly Panday began to cry again. Balraj pushed his fingers up to Panday. "How much time I tell you dat Rama not in dis wadder!"

Balraj wanted to beat Panday but he had no time to do it.

There was a loud bawling coming from the house. Ma was bawling. Then there was a noise *par par* as if dogs were running in the banana patch. Pa was running behind Ma; she was running like a horse and he was running like a big bull. Ma was getting crazy like; grabbing the banana trunks with her hands and running and laughing like a crazy woman. Pa was trying to hold her; he was trying real hard, but she was strong.

"Dis modderass woman mad!" Pa shouted.

Ma was saying all kind of things; talking out of her head like.

The black spider in the sky was coming closer to the earth. Clouds were running and piling up in a rage. The sky God was doing his work; doing it real good; just sending the clouds to choke Tola.

Ma ran out of the banana patch. She came by the riceland. She jumped into the water *ploojung!* Ma was stupid like; she ran in the mud *plaps plaps plaps*. Pa got vex. He took out the leather belt and began to beat her in the water. Then she pushed Pa; he fell down *plaps!* in the mud. Ma had a good chance to run away; instead of running away, she sat down in the water and laughed and laughed. She was playing and bathing in the nasty water. Then Pa got up and stared at her.

"You kill me son! You run him in de rain!!!" Ma shouted.

And he: "Woman you mad!"

Then Ma stood up. She pushed Pa again. He fell down *splash!* Then she bent down and started to eat a handful of mud.

"O God Ma eatin mud!" Sunaree screamed.

Balraj tried to hold her back, but Sunaree pulled her hands away. She ran through the water *splash splash splash!* to meet Ma. She ran straight to Ma and grabbed her. Ma jumped back as if Sunaree was a snake.

Hundreds of white birds were feeding on the eastern side of the riceland; they were water birds; they went *pits pits pits pits ploward ploward pits pits pits*. Doves went *tootoohoops* as they flew over the barahar tree. Small red crabs walked over the riceland bank. Where the water crossed over the meri, hundreds of black conches clung to the bamboo grass; clung like beads around a Pandit's neck.

"Ma go eat Rama in dat wadder," Panday said to Balraj.

"Shut you kiss me ass mout!" Balraj yelled. "Come on. Let we walk and go in dat riceland bank."

Balraj and Panday went and stood on the riceland bank.

Sunaree didn't move; she didn't talk or anything; she just stood there like a blacksage tree and allowed Ma to rub mud all over her. Then Ma left Sunaree and started to run toward the riceland bank.

"All you run! All you modder go bite all you!" Pa shouted.

Balraj and Panday started to run on the riceland bank;

running just to get away from Ma. But it was hard to run on the bank; it was very slippery. Ma was running in the water; they were running on the bank. Ma was running fast fast; running fast and going *splash! splash!* Then she got out of the water. She ran on the riceland bank behind Balraj and Panday. Then she grabbed Panday.

"O God! O God! Dont eat me!" Panday shouted.

Balraj didn't even look back. He knew that Ma was going to eat Panday, but he didn't even look back.

Ma just held Panday's head. She didn't say anything or do anything. She held his head for a few minutes, then she left him alone and ran behind Balraj.

Balraj was near the doodoose mango tree. He was tired like, so he looked back. Ma was running and running; running like a mule runs. When Balraj saw her he jumped up like a horse and started running *beegeedip! beegeedip!* just as a horse runs in mud. He ran until he reached Cocoa River, then he turned back and began running westward to the barahar tree. Balraj ran through the riceland and came by the banana patch. Pa, Sunaree and Panday were waiting for him.

Pa said: "All you run down Rajput Road and call all you Nanna and Nanny! Tell dem to come fast! Tell dem all you modder mad. Run! All you run!"

IX

HEAVY CLOUDS DRIFTED across the face of the sky. The whole of Tola was getting dark, but night was far away. Balraj was in front, Sunaree and Panday were just behind him. They were hungry; their bellies were going *gru gru* because they didn't eat anything all day. They walked along Tola Trace until they reached the river.

"Stop cryin and come on Panday!" Balraj shouted.

Panday was afraid because Nanna once said that there was a jables living under the bamboo crossing. The jables never interfered with little children; she never ate the children or anything. But she used to tell the duennes in Tola Forest about the children. Nanna had said that one time a jables saw a little boy walking by the river. The jables ran inside the forest and called the duennes. When the duennes came out of the silkcotton tree, the jables told them about the little boy. So the duennes came by the river and carried the little boy away.

"Boy look shut you ass and cross dat bridge!"

Balraj held on to Panday's hands and dragged him to the bamboo crossing. When they reached the middle of the crossing they saw the water underneath them. The river was deep; deep enough to cover a grass house.

"I fraid I fall!" Panday said.

"But I holdin you."

"I still fraid."

But Balraj dragged him over the bridge to the other side. When they crossed the river, Balraj stopped to look at the sky.

He was watching the clouds how they were jumping up and down in the sky; he didn't want the rain to fall; the rain was wicked like Pa; it was going to kill the tadpoles in the water just how Pa killed Rama.

They moved on. They didn't run; they just walked because they were hungry and tired. When they reached the corner of Tola Trace and Rajput Road, they heard Nanna coughing.

"Nanna!" Balraj called.

"Who is dat?"

"We Nanna," Sunaree said.

"Come nuh chirens."

Nanna sat on a potato crate. He had a white floursack tied around his head.

"Wot happen chirens?"

Nanny came out of the bedroom.

"Ma eatin mud in de riceland," Sunaree declared.

"Wot?"

"Ma get mad. She eatin mud in de cola."

Nanny remained quiet as a bandicoot, but Nanna stood up. His lips moved as if they were dying; dying as a butterfly beats its wings and dies. Nanna wanted to talk but he couldn't talk. It was as if a jumbie was upon him. Then the evil spirit left Nanna, and he said, "O God me dorta! One chile I have in dis world God . . . "

While Nanna was getting on, Nanny sat on the earthen floor; she sat like a ripe plantain or a jumbie moko. With her head in her hand she called the sky God. The sky God was rolling in blackness, but she was still calling God; calling him hard hard and telling him about her troubles. She was getting on, getting on hard hard; crying and getting on as if the sky God had any time with her. Nanny didn't know that the sky God was just a lump of blackness; she didn't know that he was dead and rotten in the sky.

Panday said, "Nanna and Nanny, all you not to get on so. Dat rain goin to fall and wash away Rama in dat riceland."

Nanna and Nanny didn't care about Panday. They continued to tell the sky God about their troubles.

"Nanna all you have to go and see Ma!" Sunaree shouted.

It was only when Sunaree shouted that Nanna and Nanny forgot the sky God. They ran out of the house; they didn't bolt the door or wait for the children; they just ran out of the house and headed up Tola Trace.

X

PA SAT LIKE a tigro snake on the potato crate. He shook his feet like two dry sticks.

Nanna and Nanny were blowing when they reached the house. When Nanna was calm enough, he asked Pa, "Wot happen to me dorta?"

"She kiss me ass mad! Dat is wot happen."

"You is a docta? How you know she mad?"

"Oldman look! I tell you she mad. She gettin on all de time since de boy dead."

"You must know dat. You is de one who get she mad."

"Shut you chamar modderass!"

Nanna said that he was not a chamar; he was a Brahmin.

"But you wife is a chamar?"

Pa shook his fist close to Nanna's face. Nanna stepped back because Pa was strong like a mango tree and Nanna was weak as a tilaree tree.

"I is a oldman," Nanna said. "Too besides I is a man of God."

And Pa: "Me eh care notten. You coud be old or young. But you kiss me ass dorta mad!"

"But where she is?" Nanny asked.

Pa didn't answer. He just shook his feet.

Nanna and Nanny looked at Pa. He watched them as if God was watching them, watching their tears and their help-lessness, watching their . . .

"Go by de doodoose mango tree and look for she!"

Nanna and Nanny went by the riceland. The thunder was coming closer and closer to the earth. Rain birds were flying low, almost touching the water. They searched the water with their eyes, but they couldn't see Ma.

"Let we go in de back and look," Nanna said.

"Oright."

They walked to the eastern end of the riceland bank, then they went by the carat tree. They called and called Ma, but there was no answer; only the thunder and the rain clouds came closer and closer to Tola.

They moved on. When they reached by the doodoose mango tree, they saw Ma. She was eating mud in the biya cola.

"Let we hold she," Nanna said to Nanny.

But they couldn't hold her. Ma ran through the riceland *flash! flash! flash!* She ran across the riceland and came out on the high land by the barahar tree.

Nanna and Nanny were afraid. They didn't want to go by the barahar tree behind Ma. They didn't want her to run from the high land into the water again, because huge water snakes lived in the riceland near the barahar tree.

Ma didn't care; she was too mad to care. She drank water from the drain near the barahar tree, pulled out bamboo grass with her hands and kicked up the dry barahar leaves with her feet.

Do dodo doom doom doomed! The thunder pounded Tola. Nanna and Nanny were afraid; Ma was by the barahar tree, but they were afraid. Tola Forest started about three hundred feet south of the barahar tree; it started just a few feet away from the long mango tree at the southern end of the riceland. Tola River ran through the forest; the river was deep. In the forest too, there were tigro snakes, coral snakes and machetes, all were deadly snakes; and beside the snakes there were the poisonous spiders, the long centipedes and the scorpions. They didn't want to go by the barahar tree because they didn't want her to run into the forest.

Balraj, Sunaree and Panday were in the kitchen, trying their best to cook something. There was a pot of rice over the fire, but the fire was giving trouble; the coconut shells were wet. Balraj took the pokanee and blew into the fire. He was blowing with all his strength; blowing so hard that all the veins in his neck bulged as earthworms. But it was no use; white smoke just piled up inside the kitchen.

"Wot de modderass all you doin in dat kitchen!" Pa shouted.

"We tryin to light de fire," Balraj said.

Pa ran inside the kitchen. He took the pot of rice and flung it in the yard. "All you know dat all you modder mad, yet all you makin smoke in de house. No food not cookin in dis house till all you modder go in dat madhouse."

Then Nanna and Nanny came back into the house. They were wet because the rain was drizzling now. They couldn't ask Pa why he threw away the rice; they were afraid to even talk to him. But they had to talk to him about Ma. So Nanny said, "Give we a hand to see about dese chirens modder."

"Wot hand all you want? De woman mad. All you cant help she now, I goin to Tolaville to get a paper to carry she in dat madhouse tomorrow."

Pa walked out of the house.

"You sure you not goin to drink rum?" Nanna asked.

"All you just wait. I goin to Tolaville to get dat paper."

Pa left for Tolaville.

Nanna and Nanny sat with the children. And Sunaree said, "Nanny dey goin to put Ma in dat madhouse. But she goin to come out. Yeh. God goin to come in de night and carry she up in dat sky. Den she and Rama goin to live in dat cloud."

"No," said Panday, as if Sunaree was talking to him. "Ma goin to live in dat madhouse. Den dey goin to cut she belly wide open. People goin to drink rum whole night. Den Ma goin to live in dat riceland wadder. I know dat."

"He lie Nanny," Sunaree said. "Ma goin to live in dat sky."

Balraj was listening all the time. He scratched his head and said, "Ma goin to live in dat madhouse till she dead. Den rat goin to eat she just how dem rats eatin Rama in Tolaville."

"All you too small to know anyting," Nanny said sadly.

The rain came down *par par par* on the grass roof. Nanna and Nanny knew that the rain wasn't going to stop; the sky was black as a black bull and the lightning was running as golden wires in the sky. They had to get Ma home; get her out of the rain and the wind. Nanny went inside the bedroom and got the drum. Without saying a word, Nanny walked out of the house with the drum. Nanna followed her.

"I not stayin in dis house," Panday said.

"Why?" Sunaree asked.

"Because I fraid a churail hold me in dis house."

Balraj, Sunaree and Panday ran out of the house; they ran on the riceland bank, trying to meet up with Nanna and Nanny. They listened. They heard the drum as it beated:

go going gone!
go going gone!
go going gone!

And the tree frogs sang:

rage raging! rage raging! rage raging!
rage raging! rage raging! rage raging!

Nanny walked slow as she beated the drum. Ma was still under the barahar tree; still pulling out bamboo grass and getting on. Then Ma heard the drum. She stood up and listened. She didn't move because the drum was beating sweeter than sugar. Nanny walked on a meri and went by the barahar tree.

Nanna kept the children on the riceland bank. He told them not to follow Nanny on the riceland bank, because they were going to make Ma run into the forest or into the deep holes in the riceland. Nanna was telling them to go back into the house, but they didn't want to go. Panday jumped from the riceland bank into the water. Then Balraj and Sunaree jumped into the water too. Balraj was dragging his hands in the water. He knew the rain was going to kill the tadpoles; he wanted to catch some to put in the hole by the coconut tree.

"All you come outa dat wadder chirens!" Nanna shouted.

They didn't want to come out. Nanna took a lump of mud and flung it in the water. He said, "All you come outa dat wadder. A snake just jump in dat wadder."

Balraj, Sunaree and Panday came and stood on the riceland bank.

"Now all you go on home chirens."

"But we fraid Nanna," Panday said.

"All you go home befo all you modder bite all you."

They walked home slowly.

Nanny didn't look back or anything; she just kept her eyes on the ground as she beated the drum. Nanny beated the drum to the barahar tree. When she reached by Ma she just turned around and walked back with the drum; she walked on the meri until she came on the riceland bank; she walked on to meet the house. Ma followed her. Nanny beated the drum until she reached in the house. Ma came into the house too;

her eyes moved all over the place. Her hair was full of dirt, and bluish mud stuck to her dress. Nanny beated and beated the drum, and Ma danced all the time.

"Put dem chirens inside de kitchen," Nanny said to Nanna. "We have to change she clothes."

While Nanna was hurrying Balraj, Sunaree and Panday into the kitchen, Nanny unstrung the drum from around her neck. She placed the drum on the ground and looked at Ma. When Nanny was sure that Ma wasn't going to run away, she went inside the house and got an old dress for Ma. She had to look real good in the cardboard box, because most of the clothes in the house were wet. When she came out of the bedroom, Nanna was waiting for her by the tapia wall.

"Where dem chirens? I not hearin dem."

"Dem in de kitchen. I tell dem to stay quiet," Nanna said.

Nanny turned to Ma. "Take out you dress. We want to bathe you."

Ma stood by the tapia wall and laughed all the time.

Nanna and Nanny laughed with her, because they didn't want her to run away. Then they ripped off her dress *purr purr*. Nanny dipped her hands in the bucket and bathed her. Then they wiped her skin dry with an old floursack and slipped on a clean dress over her.

Ma said, "De bull buttin de chile. All you look! De man runnin dat chile in de rain. Fire lightnin in de sky . . . "

Rain clouds stood over Tola like a pool of black water. Nanna and Nanny brought Ma inside the kitchen; they told the children to go inside the bedroom.

Then night covered Tola with a web. Balraj, Sunaree and Panday were asleep in the bedroom. Ma was asleep on the old bags in the kitchen. Nanny slept next to her. Nanna sat up by the doorway. But the night moved on like a snail that brought slime and sleep into their eyes; layers and layers of blackness choked the earth; Tola breathed *soot soot soot* as the wind and the rain pounded the earth. The light was out, because the night pounded the house and pounded the light also. Nanna woke up. He felt for the light. He lit the flambeau. Fear came upon him: Ma was gone; she had emptied her bowels in the kitchen and disappeared into the darkness. Nanna bawled out, "Getup! Getup!!!"

Nanny sat up with sleep in her eyes. "Uh! Uh!"

"Wake up!!!"

Nanny jumped up. She picked up Ma's waste in her hand. "I trowin dis mud in de yard."

And Nanna: "Dat is shit you holdin. She messup and gone away in de night."

Nanny opened her eyes wide. Then she took the waste and walked out of the house; she didn't take it and fling it away in the wind and the rain; she just walked with it to the running water, and put it in the running water. When she came back to the house, she asked Nanna, "You see wen she gone oldman?"

"No," Nanna said. "I de tired. I fall asleep. Wen I get up and light de light, she de done gone outa de house."

And Nanny: "O God! Maybe she done drownd in de river!"

Nanna woke up the children. He told them to run out into the darkness and look for Ma. They said they were afraid.

"All you have to go up Tola Trace to Karan Settlement and Lima Road. All you have to go and look for all you modder. All you not have to fraid notten."

They hesitated.

"All you go!" Nanna shouted.

Balraj, Sunaree and Panday walked out of the house.

Nanna and Nanny went by the riceland to look for Ma. They didn't carry the light, because the rain and the wind were too strong. There were all kind of noises coming from inside the dark mouth of the night. The thunder went:

cratax cratax doom doom doomed!

The water flowed over the riceland bank:

trouble trouble trouble!
trouble trouble trouble!

The night birds sang:

ah! ah! ah!
ah! ah! ah!
ah! ah! ah!

The wind passed over the riceland:

hush hush hushing!
hush hush hushing!

Nanna and Nanny walked and walked and called and called, but the darkness swallowed their voices like a snake.

Balraj, Sunaree and Panday walked through the bamboo and basmatia grass until they came out where Karan Settlement and Lima Road met. They called but they couldn't hear Ma.
There was a noise *ssh ssh* in the bamboo grass. They stood and watched. A white dog came out of the grass. When the dog saw them it ran away.
"Dat is a lagahu!" Panday shouted.
"Dat is a dog!" Balraj shouted.
"But I fraid."

"Wot you fraid?"

And Sunaree said, "Dat is a lagahu Balraj. Nanna tell we one time dat lagahu does turn to dog. Dat is a lagahu. I fraid!"

And Balraj: "All you not have to fraid notten!"

"But sappose it is a lagahu?" Panday asked.

Sunaree remembered something. "If dat is a lagahu it cant do we notten. Rama in de sky. He go beat dat lagahu."

And Balraj: "Rama dead and all you stupid. Wen a crappo fish dead, it dead. It finish. Dat is all."

Sunaree and Panday told Balraj that they were not looking for Ma any more. They were afraid of the lagahu, because one time Nanna told them that a man in Karan Settlement used to turn to a dog. The man was working for the Devil. The Devil used to ride him through the village in the night. Sometimes the Devil used to turn the man into a white dog.

"Oright," Balraj said. "We goin back home."

They were wet and cold and hungry. They turned back and headed for home.

Nanna and Nanny walked on the riceland bank, then they took a meri and went by the barahar tree. Ma was not there. They walked to the long mango tree. She was not there either. They decided to go into the forest and look for her. Nanny sang and called as they walked through the forest; she sang and called until they came to the river. The water was high and the river sang *gulp gulp gulp!*

"It hard to find she on a night like dis," Nanna said.

The lightning danced over their heads like golden forks and silver spoons and the thunder rolled and rolled and rolled as if the sky God was beating heavy drums in the sky. The rain fell as vomit on the trees in the forest and the water made the earth cold and muddy.

"Go back in de house and get de drum," Nanna said.

Nanny left Nanna in the forest and went back to the house for the brown hand drum. While she was looking for the drum in the dark Balraj, Sunaree and Panday came home.

"All you see all you modder?"

"No Nanny," Balraj said.

"All you look good?"

"Yeh Nanny," Panday said. "We look till we see a lagahu."

Then Nanny got the drum. She told them to stay at home, but they wanted to go with her; they were afraid to stay at home. Nanny walked with the drum into the night; they followed her like dogs. And Nanny beated the drum slowly:

doom doom doomed!
doom doom doomed!

Then she beated faster:

bamboo patcha! banga patcha!
bamboo patcha! banga patcha!
bamboo patcha! banga patcha!
go going gone!
go going gone!
go going gone!

Nanny beated the drum with life; with love; she beated the drum with all her strength and the drum sounded loud as if a spirit was bawling in the forest.

The sky twisted like a black snake and the clouds rolled and rolled and rolled as a big spider; the wind shook Tola in a rage and the rain pounded the earth; the lightning came out of the mouth of the darkness like a golden tongue and licked the trees in the forest and the drum ripped through the darkness like a knife. They moved deeper and deeper into the forest, and they felt the rain falling upon their heads from heaven.

GLOSSARY

Arti: a fundamental part of almost every Brahminical rite, in which a diya is set on a taria, lit, and moved with circular gestures.

Baba: a Hindu priest, usually a member of the highest (Brahmin) caste.

Bandicoot: large rat.

Beti: daughter.

Bhajans: hymns.

Biya kola: a small plot of riceland with rice seedlings.

Chamar: one who belongs to the lowest of the four castes. The majority of Indians who came from India to work on the sugar plantations between 1845 and 1917 were chamars.

Change: tether.

Chila: fire-stick.

Churail: a spirit of purely Indian origin. It is believed to be the restless soul of a woman who died during pregnancy or childbirth. Its malicious mission on earth is to haunt the wife and children of its former husband.

Cola: (*See* meri.)

Crappo: frog.

Crappo fish: tadpoles.

Creole: a Negro born on Carib Island.

Cutlass: blade used for cutting sugar cane.

Dal (or dahl): yellow split peas. Dal and rice is the staple food of the East Indians in Carib Island.

Diya (or deeya): small earthen vessel. During Hindu ceremonies, coconut oil is placed inside the diya, then a small cotton wick is inserted and lit by a priest or devotee. The flame is recognised as holy fire.

Duenne: a spirit of African origin. Duennes are the spirits of children who die before they are born. The heels of the foetus-spirits are in front, and the toes are turned backwards. These tiny spirit creatures dwell in small communities deep in the forest.

Flambeau: a torch. A flambeau is made by putting kerosene into an empty beer bottle and inserting a cloth wick.

Jables: (corruption of the French term diablesse, or female devil). A witch, or agent of the devil, who takes the shape of a beautiful woman. People in the countryside believe that the jables has one normal human foot and one cloven. Keeping the normal foot on the road and the cloven one in the grass, she lures men who travel at night along country roads to their destruction.

Jamet: whore.

Jumbie: spirit. People in the country believe that mysterious creatures lurk around the villages at night. The term is of widespread use in the Caribbean: some people believe jumbies are sent by obeahmen (sorcerers), while others think of a jumbie as the soul of a departed person. The latter belief is particularly strong among the Indians.

Jumbie bird: owl. The Indians in Carib Island believe that if an owl sits on a rooftop and hoots, someone in the family will die soon.

Lagahu: (corruption of the French term loup garou, or werewolf). A living person who has made contact with the devil. Through supernatural prayers he takes the form of an animal at night. The devil pays him a sum of money and rides him through the village.

Lota: brass cup.

Madrassi: all black, or dark-skinned East Indians. The term is used loosely; black East Indians came from Ceylon as well as the state of Madras.

Mantras: prayers.

Meri: a low straight bank in the riceland, usually built to control the water in the cola. The meris meet at right angles, forming plots; these plots are colas (or kolas).

Nursery: seedling.

Orhni: headshawl worn by married Indian women. Today it is worn mostly in the countryside. Indian women who live in cities and towns refuse to wear the orhni because they have become "too creolised."

Pandit: a Hindu priest. Only a Brahmin (one who belongs to the highest caste) can validly become a Hindu priest. During the period 1845 to 1917, very few Brahmins came to Carib Island from India. Many men of lower caste were known to go to other villages and set themselves up as Brahmin priests, thereby escaping the hard work on the plantations.

Quenck: wild hog.

Roti: unleavened bread.

Saddhu: a Hindu ascetic, or one who lives in a temple. A Saddhu usually belongs to a lower caste, and so cannot become a pandit.

Silkcotton tree: a tree that is the ideal abode for spirits. Superstition has it that if a silkcotton tree is struck with an axe, blood spurts out. Jumbies also live in mango, neem, and calabash trees.

Taria: a brass plate.

Tola: village, settlement.

Trace: unpaved road, mud path.

Anansi Fiction

The Wabeno Feast
by Wayland Drew

When an environmental disaster destroys Toronto, four childhood friends are forced to choose the extremes by which they will survive. One man, Paul Henry, returns to the Northern Ontario of his youth, seeking to escape and endure deep within the wilderness.

"An astonishing accomplishment . . ." – M. T. Kelly
0-88784-6637

Awake When All the World Is Asleep
by Shree Ghatage

It is the 1970s, and Shaila has returned to Bombay for her father's sixtieth birthday party. A whole rich world opens up as Shree Ghatage lovingly articulates daily life in India's urban south in this lively, humorous, poignant collection.

"A stunning achievement . . . a gifted and original writer." – Toronto Star
0-88784-6025

Spirits in the Dark
by H. Nigel Thomas

Jerome Quashee is paralyzed within a maze of social pressures growing up in the Caribbean. He wrestles with his emerging homosexuality, with the guilt of knowing so little about his African heritage, and above all with the pressure to leave behind his own culture – to speak, think, and act "white" in order to proceed in the world.

". . . a vivid and convincing portrayal . . . of Caribbean society." – Books in Canada
0-88784-5355

The Plight of Happy People in an Ordinary World
by Natalee Caple

Nadja and Irma are working in their family bakery when Josef walks in one day, initiating a double seduction that will change the course of all their lives. Everyone is forced to examine the problem of their own happiness while the physical world manifests the awesome complications of the heart.

"Caple's writing has a taut, dreamlike quality." – THIS magazine
0-88784-6335

Available at fine bookstores and at www.anansi.ca